THE BETRAYERS

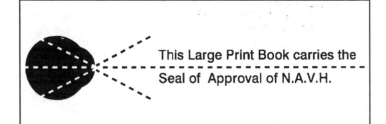

This Large Print Book carries the
Seal of Approval of N.A.V.H.

THE BETRAYERS

JAMES PATRICK HUNT

THORNDIKE PRESS

An imprint of Thomson Gale, a part of The Thomson Corporation

THOMSON

GALE

Detroit • New York • San Francisco • New Haven, Conn. • Waterville, Maine • London

THOMSON

GALE

™

LIBRARY OF CONGRESS CATALOGING-IN-PUBLICATION DATA

Hunt, James Patrick, 1964–
   The betrayers / by James Patrick Hunt.
      p. cm. — (Thorndike Press large print core)
   ISBN-13: 978-0-7862-9513-5 (alk. paper)
   ISBN-10: 0-7862-9513-9 (alk. paper)
   1. Police — Missouri — Saint Louis — Fiction. 2. Saint Louis (Mo.) —
Fiction. 3. Large type books. I. Title.
PS3608.U577B48 2007b
813'.6—dc22   2007008286

Published in 2007 by arrangement with St. Martin's Press, LLC.

Printed in the United States of America on permanent paper
10 9 8 7 6 5 4 3 2 1

To my nieces,
all of them

There is the fact that treason is an attempt to live without love of country, which humanity can't do — any more than love of family.

— Rebecca West

ACKNOWLEDGMENTS

The author wishes to express his gratitude to his editor, Kelley Ragland, and his agent, David Hale Smith, for believing in a relative newcomer.

The author is also grateful to a number of police officers who have assisted him over the years on matters of procedure and technique as well as offering guidance on cop culture. These officers include but are not limited to Darrell Hatfield, Greg Cunningham, Mike Denton, Burl Cox, Ray Aldridge, John Roberts, and Justin Humphreys. They have helped me learn that police departments have a handful of rogues and a handful of saints, depending on what day you drop by, but that the majority of those who take the oath are decent people trying to serve their communities.

ONE

The two county deputies sat in the front seats of the patrol car watching the guy they had pulled over standing in the glow of the headlights, giving them his profile, standing still as he was told to, but clenching and unclenching his fists because he was scared and stoned and it was hard to remain in one place.

The deputies had pulled him over a few minutes earlier because he had been doing forty-three in a thirty-five.

Deputy Chris Hummel had called the dispatcher at 2043 hours and advised they had stopped a 1999 Chevy Suburban with a license tag number KAY-6705 and then got out of the car to talk to the young man. Asked him a few questions, then got back in to discuss with his young partner what they should do next. It was Hummel who was driving.

The dispatcher came back. She ran the

driver's license number and tag and did not find any outstanding warrants or record on the guy.

Deputy Hummel said, "Son of a bitch." Disappointed. He said to the patrol officer next to him, "Look at him. Is he not blazed out?"

Deputy Wade Childers said, "Yeah. Look at his hands."

Night. Cold out, a fine mist that was not going to become rain anytime soon. Early November. There was hip-hop playing on the radio in the patrol car. The windshield wipers slapped intermittently between them and the guy that had been requested to step out of his vehicle and stand in front of the patrol car.

The deputies were both in their twenties; Childers on the low end, Hummel on the upper end. It was Hummel's eighth year in law enforcement; cynical and hard-bitten, but not yet tired. Hummel was married with two children. The older child had been from his wife's first marriage; Hummel had adopted him a year after he married the boy's mother. They had the second child together. He was taking two courses at the University of Missouri–Saint Louis and he hoped to have his bachelor's degree in criminal justice by the time he was thirty.

Deputy Wade Childers was twenty-four and looked it. He was not married, but he had a serious girlfriend whom he had known since he was fourteen. Childers had been a law enforcement officer for ten months. It was his rookie year; he was still on probation. Like many young men, he was drawn to the trappings, the *stuff,* of law enforcement. The uniform, the cars, the guns, the handcuffs, the OC spray, the batons and ASPs; what Chris Hummel liked to call "the fuckin' *tools.*"

Childers was also attracted to the rush of police work, the downright narcotic effect of racing to the scene of a crime: a fire, a shooting, a robbery. It did not matter so much what the event was; what mattered was that there was an event happening now and you were going to be there. You were going to be there and you were going to handle it because no one else would know how. It is this rush that peels young men away from other professions that pay better wages, that set more reasonable working hours, that are more hospitable to marriage and family, that are devoid of opportunities of being shot at or sued or terminated at the whim of a shift captain who thinks your wedding tackle might be bigger than his. Wade Childers, at twenty-four, did not contemplate the hazards to the psyche that come with police work. He did not think about paranoia or burnout or stress from being witness to violence and death and cruelty and injustice. He did not think about administrative backbiting and politics and callous bureaucracy. Wade Childers thought police work was cool and pitied those who did not have the opportunity to do what he did. Wade Childers was, in short, a very young police officer.

They were parked in a lot off Manchester Road in St. Louis County. Cars whisked by, slowing by degrees as they passed the stationary police car with the flashing red and blue lights. There was an Ace Hardware store and a Dollar General store nearby, both of them closed for the night.

Chris Hummel said, "He's a big old boy."

The man standing in the November mist *was* big. Much bigger and heavier than Chris Hummel. But if the man in the headlights felt any size advantage over Deputy Hummel he never showed it. If he ever felt it at all, it was forgotten when Hummel made him step out of the car and explain who he was and where he was going. Hummel stood about five-nine and weighed no more than 165 pounds, but he had the voice and the stance and the body language that intimidated people. Watching him, rookie Wade Childers — who was also physically bigger than Hummel — felt envy and admiration. How? How do you learn to do that? Are you just born with it?

Truth be told, in his years of police work, Deputy Hummel had pulled his service weapon from his holster only once. That had been when he saw a man reach into the backseat of his car to reach for a shiny object that Hummel had thought was a shotgun. There followed a lot of screaming and shouting of orders and warnings and the man got out of the car and facedown on the ground. The thing he had been reaching for turned out to be an aluminum baseball bat. Hummel was thankful he had not killed the man.

Deputy Hummel was no pacifist. Like most police officers not on the executive board of a police union, he was the sort of right-wing Republican that establishment Republicans prefer to keep in the background. Hummel, for example, opposed sending conventional troops into Iraq because he believed it would have been easier — and, from his perspective, more humane — just to flatten the rebel hot spots with two or three nuclear bombs in as many days and start from scratch. But armchair politics

15

aside, he possessed good street instincts. He knew when to use the appropriate level of force and when not to and, if necessary, when to run like hell.

His instincts told him now that the man in the headlights was a turd and a bump monkey looking for the kick that comes with snorting methamphetamine. Given the right encouragement, the man would probably be able to lead them to a meth kitchen.

Hummel said, "I can smell it on him."

Childers said, "Well, what do you want to do?"

"I don't know." Hummel said, "Look at his shirt."

"Yeah. What is that?"

They could see a brown patch on the man's white tennis shirt.

Hummel said, "That's what I asked. He said he burned a hole in it." Deputy Hummel sighed. "Look at him. I don't know if he's high or retarded. . . . What, what is he doing now? Is he singing?"

"Yeah. He's singing."

"Goddamn."

"Look at his hands. Fucking tensed up."

"Yeah. Big-time."

"I'm waiting for him to fall over. Looks like he's going to pass out."

"Shit, he's only been standing there for

five minutes."

"Yeah, but he'll tell people later it was two hours."

After a moment, Deputy Hummel said, "We don't have anything on him."

The young man in the headlights still seemed to be singing or humming to himself. Facing the road, his left profile to the deputies behind the patrol car's windshield.

Hummel said to Childers, "Wonder if I can sneak out of the car, walk up behind him real quiet, scare the shit out of him."

That's what he did. Deputy Wade Childers remained in the patrol car, watching the performance, Chris Hummel creeping up right behind the guy like he was coming on to him. Wade Childers smiled as he saw Chris speak into the man's left ear, then laughed as he saw the man jump in fright — who's that? — Chris keeping the same deadpan expression beneath his cap the whole time. Chris talked with the guy a little while longer before letting him get in the Suburban and go home. And again Wade Childers wondered how Deputy Hummel did it.

Hummel got back in the patrol car, radioed dispatch to 10-8, and drove back out into traffic.

They drove at a leisurely pace down

Manchester Road, controlling the traffic ahead and behind them as other drivers warily kept their speed below posted limits and their beer cans out of sight. The patrol car passed the colors and lights of American commerce: video rentals, fast food restaurants, supermarkets with blue and white fronts.

Hummel's cell phone rang and he answered it.

Childers did not look over because he did not want Chris to think he was eavesdropping, even though he was. It was night shift and there were long stretches of boredom to get through. He could not hear what the caller was saying, but Chris was distinct.

"Uh-huh . . . uh-huh . . . uh-huh. I under-*stand* that. . . . Babe, there's nothing I can do about it right now. . . . Nothing I can do about it right now. . . . Huh? . . . I don't remember the black pattern. . . . No, I still don't. . . . Okay . . . Then do that. . . . Okay. Bye."

Hummel put the cellular phone back in his coat pocket.

"That was my wife," he said. "She's pissed at me."

Childers did not feel it was his place to ask why, so he just said, "Yeah?"

Hummel said, "We're redecorating the

18

fuckin' house. Kitchen." He sighed. "Fuckin' cabinets." He said the word like it was a disease. "You ever get cabinets installed?"

Wade Childers said, "No."

"Don't fuckin' get me started on cabinets. They start talking about cabinets, just bend over and grab your ankles."

"You mean it's expensive?"

"Expensive? It's like getting hit by a swarm of locusts. They take everything."

"They . . . you mean the contractors."

"Yeah. Assisted dutifully by my wife."

Young Wade Childers said, "Can't you just say no?"

Deputy Hummel was actually made anxious by this question. He had opened the door by revealing his frustration to the younger police officer who he knew looked up to him. He was Wade's field training officer (FTO) and he had to retain the younger officer's respect. Would the young man think that tough guy Chris Hummel let his wife push him around? He would have to set this straight right now.

Hummel said, "Man, what planet are you on? You think I want to be divorced? Separated from my kids? You get married, have a family, this is the shit you have to do. Let me tell you how it works: six months ago, I

19

bought that Kawasaki Ninja bike. Nothing fancy. 2001 model. Paid four grand for it. Good deal, right? Well, that motorcycle is going to end up costing me about forty thousand dollars before it's all through. Know why? Because the old lady looks at it and says, okay, now it's time for *me* to get something. But — and this is what women do — she says that, unlike my motorcycle, the kitchen remodeling is for *all of us.* It's not a *selfish* gift, she says. I get a bike, she gets fucking cabinets. And they cost about ten times more than the fuckin' bike." A pause as Wade Childers laughed. "It's not funny."

Then a car passed them on their left, going at least seventy on a city street. A Nissan Pathfinder, it swerved back in front of them after going by, making Hummel touch the brakes; they heard its tires squeal and watched it move away from them.

"Jesus!" Deputy Childers said.

Hummel said, "Rock and roll," switched on the lights and siren, and pressed the accelerator to the floor.

And there it was: the rush of a pursuit. Lights flashing, siren blaring, the road approaching them, rising and falling like a screen on a video game. A kick, the prospect of sudden quarry, the determined thrill the

20

dog feels from his nostrils to his chest chasing the rabbit.

Childers radioed dispatch to tell them they were in pursuit of a Nissan Pathfinder, with a license tag not yet determined. They caught up with it and put the lights on full beam into the back windows.

The vehicle slowed.

Childers said, "Now he sees us."

Hummel said, "He's stoned. Or drunk."

The Nissan Pathfinder continued to decelerate. But it kept going. Like he was on his way to a funeral, the police escorting him from behind.

Hummel said, "What is this fucking guy's problem? Pull over, son of a bitch."

The Pathfinder continued for another half mile.

Hummel flashed the brights on and off, light filling the back of the vehicle ahead, knowing the effect it had on a typical drunk driver, filling him with fear.

The Pathfinder made a right turn onto a side street, away from the traffic and lights, the patrol car right on its tail. Finally the Pathfinder slowed to a stop and the patrol car stopped behind it.

Wade Childers had mixed feelings. The excitement of the chase still with him, he was sorry it ended too soon. A drunk, that was all it was.

Both of the deputies got out of the patrol car and approached the vehicle, Hummel going up to the driver's side, Childers walking up the passenger's side. They reached the front of the vehicle and saw the man behind the wheel. He looked to be around forty.

Hummel said, "Evening, sir." Using his tone of authority that was above speaking level but not quite shouting.

"What?" the man said. He did not seem terribly upset about being pulled over.

Hummel looked directly at him, pausing for effect, then saying, "You in a hurry?"

"What?" the man said. "Was I speeding or something?"

Hummel regarded the man behind the wheel. Thick, dark hair, dated sideburns . . . turd air about him. Hummel thought, street. Menace. Hummel could sense it the way experienced cops sense such things.

"Slick," Hummel said, "I don't know that I'd call that speeding. More like reckless driving. Step out of the vehicle."

"Awww, fuck," the man said. "Come on."

"Now."

The man opened the door and got out. He looked over at Childers, waiting for him to move. He did. He came around the front of the Pathfinder past the driver and stood next to Hummel. The man kept his hands at his sides.

Hummel said, "You been drinking?"

"No, I haven't been fuckin' drinkin'."

Hummel said, "You stoned?"

"What?"

"Are . . . you . . . stoned?" Hummel said, giving him his Adam West delivery.

"Man, why're ya fuckin' ridin' me?"

Hummel said, "You want to watch the language, Slick? We can cuff you, and get out the Tasers and go to work, you push it hard enough."

The man almost seemed to smile.

"Hey," the man said, holding his hands up in a conciliatory gesture. "I was just driving, you know."

"We've established that you were driving," Hummel said. "My question is —"

A black Pontiac Bonneville drove up and came to a quick stop behind them. The driver of the Pathfinder stepped back, and kept stepping back. The deputies heard the Pontiac's engine, the tires scrunching to a halt, and then looked to their left and saw it, but did not believe what they saw, because it was happening before they knew it: A man in the backseat of the Pontiac, no more than eight feet away from them, pointing a stubby machine gun out the back window and pulling the trigger, shooting rounds into the deputies before they could utter a word or reach for the sidearms. The roar of gunfire burst in the dark, lighting up as the slugs poured into the deputies, cutting and twisting them, slamming them back against the Pathfinder.

The gunfire ceased.

The driver of the Pathfinder walked to the front passenger door of the Pontiac and got in. He shut the door and the car accelerated away.

Two

The engine was roaring as it accelerated as if the men behind them would get up off the ground, rising like zombies, and unload buckshot through the back window. But they were dead — they had seen it happen — they were dead and there was no point in jamming the accelerator in the getaway like a bunch of fucking hopped-up junkies after their first stickup. Panicking. That's what the driver was doing, and he was going to get them all hooked or killed.

"Christ!" Jimmy said. "You just ran another fuckin' stop sign!"

"I'm sorry —"

"Do you *want* to get popped? Slow the fuck down."

"Sorry —"

"Don't say you're sorry; just do it."

The kid, whose name was Eddie Cunningham, gripped the steering wheel like he was hanging from it. He didn't know if the man next to him had a gun on him now. He had seen Jimmy with guns before. In a storeroom at the back of a bar and grill, Eddie had once seen Jimmy stick a gun in a guy's mouth. Eddie thought it was funny then. The guy with the gun in his mouth had gone double or nothing on a Lakers' game, lost, and was tardy with the payment. The amount owed was eight hundred dollars — pocket money for them — but these guys were serious about having debts paid. Jimmy let the guy go so he could come back the next day with the money plus another hundred, apology money. Too bad; Eddie had never seen a guy get shot through the mouth.

From the backseat, Dillon said, "Jimmy, relax, will ya? You're makin' it worse. Eddie, just drive like we're going home from a ball game."

Eddie Cunningham slowed the car down for the next stop sign. They were still in a residential neighborhood, dark and tree lined. A narrow street with cars parked on the sides, the brick houses set close to each other.

Dillon said, "That's better."

Dillon looked into the rearview mirror. Nothing. He slipped the machine gun into a black leather bag. He closed the bag and slipped it behind his feet.

Eddie made a right turn onto another neighborhood street, more stop signs. Just signs, but he was approaching them like they were checkpoints now. Slow and cautious. Finally they crept out of the residential area and turned north on Watson Road. Took that to Litzinger and went west on that until they reached 67. Eddie stopped at the light, waited for the traffic light, and turned north again. He drove above the speed limit, but made sure he was not going faster than the other cars. He blended in. Going home from a game.

Jimmy Rizza lit a cigarette. Using the electric switch, he cracked the window. He held the cigarette in his right hand, resting his elbow on the armrest. The breeze caught the smoke and pulled it out of the car. No rain got in, but they could feel the cool and the moisture inside and hear the sounds of night traffic.

Dillon said, "Feeling better now, Jimmy?"

"Yeah. I'm okay now."

It was a joke between them. One time in a bar in Chicago, an off-duty state trooper had called Jimmy a mick — Jimmy's mother was Irish — and Jimmy had exploded. Dillon pulled him out of the bar before he killed the trooper and got them all pinched. Once outside, Dillon and his friends had calmed Jimmy down, persuaded him that mick was a term of endearment. "Not from someone like him," Jimmy said. A few minutes passed and Jimmy lit a cigarette and looked at the bar window and said, "Okay, I feel better now." Making fun of himself, maybe.

Now Dillon said, "You're doing good, Eddie. Right, Jimmy?"

In the front seat, Jimmy Rizza turned and looked at Eddie. "Yeah," Jimmy said. "I'm sorry I yelled at ya. I got a bad temper. It's nothin' personal."

"It's all right," Eddie said.

"It was those fuckin' cops," Jimmy said. "Got me all riled up."

Dillon said, "Yeah?"

"Yeah. Callin' me 'slick.' "

After a moment in which no one spoke, Eddie said, "That ain't right."

Thirty-five minutes later, Eddie wheeled the Pontiac into the parking lot of an abandoned racquetball club in Bridgeton. There were two other cars in the lot: a black Oldsmobile that, from a distance, looked similar to the Pontiac and a green two-door Jeep Cherokee. Eddie parked the Pontiac a few yards from the Olds.

Jimmy looked at the Cherokee. "That your car?"

"Yeah," Eddie said.

Jimmy threw his cigarette out the window, pressed the electric switch, and closed it.

Jimmy said, "You weren't supposed to park it here. You were supposed to park it someplace away from here and walk to it."

"It was raining when I got here," Eddie said.

In the backseat, Mike Dillon took a .22 revolver from his jacket pocket, put it to the back of Eddie's head, and pulled the trigger. Eddie slumped forward and Dillon put another four bullets into his head.

Dillon said, "Help me put him in the trunk, uh?"

"Yeah," Jimmy said. "You got shovels?"

"In the Olds." Dillon sighed. The mist was still with them. Dillon considered himself. He was in good shape; he still worked out with weights, watched what he ate, avoided second helpings. At fifty, he still had the flat stomach he'd had when he was a twenty-five-year-old prison inmate. Still strong, but fifty now, and he could feel it in his legs and back when he got out of bed in the morning.

"Well," Dillon said, "at least the ground will be soft."

29

THREE

In the same hour that the two policemen were murdered, two other police officers were in a room in Barnes-Jewish Hospital. One of them, George Hastings, sat in a visitor's chair reading a *People* magazine; the other, Joseph Klosterman, lay in the bed, recuperating from surgery. Both of them were homicide detectives for the St. Louis police department; Hastings, a lieutenant, Klosterman, his sergeant.

On many levels, they were quite different men. Klosterman was big in the chest and shoulders and he wore a thick mustache. Because he was a detective, he had not worn a uniform in years. But anyone looking at him would guess that he was a policeman. Which was fine with Klosterman. A policeman was all he had ever really wanted to be. He was raised in a cop family. Dad, uncles, cousins — there were many Klostermans in law enforcement. He liked to tell jokes and stories . . . liked performing. His bearing and common use of the standard cop profanity — turd, douche, fucker, and motherfucker — belied his absolute devotion to his wife and children. People who knew him well noticed that Joe Klosterman never used the vulgar language in front of his wife or children and he was a regular churchgoer. This dichotomy is not uncommon with policemen or soldiers. He was in his middle thirties, but he looked older.

George Hastings, in contrast, was quiet by nature. A good listener, which is important for a detective. He was thinner and shorter than the sergeant and he had never worn a mustache. Unlike Joe and most of the other detectives on their squad, Hastings did not take much of an interest in sports. He did not keep track of how many games the Rams won and lost. But it was Hastings who had the athletic background. He had once been a promising baseball player and had attended Saint Louis University on a full athletic scholarship. A knee injury in his last year of college had put an end to any real thought of a professional baseball career and when he graduated with a degree in something called communications, he found he was without any serious prospects. He did know that he did not want to return to

Nebraska and work in a meatpacking plant.

So he tended bar at a place called Jack Taylor's, one of the West County clubs with an eighteen-month shelf life where the owners never paid taxes and didn't like customers who asked a lot of questions. The job wasn't bad. It was a great way to meet girls and the money was okay in the short term. But it was unsatisfying work. He didn't enjoy making small talk with the customers and he was particularly depressed by the notion of becoming the proverbial ex-jock bartender. You could only stretch the game so far.

One day, Hastings arrived at the bar to find that it had been robbed. Money had been removed from the safe and from other places he didn't know about. He was interviewed by a detective about the robbery. It turned out the detective was from Omaha. The two of them talked about a Nebraska-Oklahoma game they both had seen that pissed them off and their mutual admiration for coach Tom Osborne before the detective, with some apparent reluctance, moved onto questions about the break-in. After the questions, the detective looked around to see if anyone was listening, then lowered his voice before speaking again.

He said, "You seem like an all right guy,

unlike most of the turds associated with this place. So I'm gonna tell you something and I want you to listen real close: *it's really not a good idea for you to be working here.*" The detective looked at Hastings then in a way that left no doubt that the owners of Jack Taylor's were into some dirty shit. Hastings did not follow up with any questions of his own, but the look on the detective's face scared him enough that he resigned the next day. He took care not to offend Jack when he did it, because Jack had always been good to him. Hastings had wanted to quit sooner or later anyway and he did not think he was going to get a better sign that the time was right than the expression on that detective's face.

A few months after he quit, Jack Taylor was arrested and charged with a litany of crimes including but not limited to drug trafficking.

Then a couple of months after that, Hastings ran into the detective. They were standing in line at the Kenrick movie theater, Hastings with a date, waiting to see a movie. Weird. The detective seemed different in that setting; standing with his wife, wearing shorts and a T-shirt, looking like a high school coach. Hastings thanked him for what he had done and the two ended up talking about police work in general. Hastings expressed an interest in it, particularly that sort of police work where you got to use your head. The detective said, "You understand that you don't get to be a detective right away. You have to put years in on the street, on patrol. And even after years of that, there's no guarantee."

Hastings said he understood that and the next week, took the entrance exam.

That was sixteen years ago.

A lot had happened since then: marriage, a moderately successful career at the Department, fatherhood, divorce.

Hastings was thirty-nine now, older than Klosterman. It was the younger policeman who was now in the hospital bed, looking older and frightfully thin. They had removed a tumor the size of a softball from Klosterman's stomach and then afterward told him it was benign. For several days up till then, Klosterman had believed he was going to die.

Klosterman said, "The doctor says I should be back to work in four to six weeks."

Hastings thought, yeah, maybe. And with about forty pounds back on. Jesus, Klosterman was thin. Hastings had been scared too and hoped he had succeeded in hiding his fear. He said, "That's great news. The sooner you get back, the sooner I can get rid of your replacement."

The replacement was Sergeant Robert Cain. And Hastings truly did not like him. But he wanted to lift Joe's spirits too, showing no doubt that he would be back.

Klosterman said, "You holding up all right?"

"What?" Hastings said. "You mean the divorce?"

"Yeah."

"Yeah, I'm all right. Eileen agreed to joint custody."

"Yeah?" Klosterman seemed unsure. He and his wife had never liked Eileen Hastings, had always suspected that she would leave George for another man — another man with a hell of a lot more money — which is exactly what she did. But they also knew that George had genuinely loved her, for reasons they could not comprehend, and would not heal anytime soon.

"Hey," Hastings said, "you're the one in the fucking hospital."

"Yeah, I know. But Annie worries about you."

"Well, tell her not to worry. Eileen could have fought me on custody of Amy and she didn't."

Still defending her, Klosterman thought.

Well, it was what it was. He said, "But you adopted Amy."

Hastings said, "Of course I did." And Klosterman decided to let it drop.

Hastings looked out the window at the hotel across the street. At the intersection of Forest Park Parkway and Kingshighway below, cars were descending down a small tunnel underneath the boulevard and coming out the other side into Forest Park. The cars' headlights cut fuzzy beams into the nighttime mist.

Klosterman said, "Christ, I'm depressed."

"It's natural," Hastings said.

"What?"

"It's natural. When you have a death scare, you get depressed about it. Didn't your doctor talk to you about it?"

"Maybe," Klosterman said. "I don't remember. You'd think I'd be used to it. Death, I mean. Because of the work."

"It's not your death you investigate."

"No, I guess not."

"You having second thoughts?"

"About what?"

"I don't know. About coming back to work?"

"Coming back to work?"

"Yeah."

"No, I don't think so."

"No, you're not having second thoughts?"

"I am not having second thoughts," Klosterman said. "I look forward to coming back to work."

Hastings felt a modicum of shame. It had been a selfish line of questioning on his part. Joe Klosterman was one of the few friends he had; it made work easier. Hastings had no plans to resign if Klosterman did not come back, but his absence would change his perspective about the job. It would make the drive to work longer. He felt relieved to get confirmation. Having received it, he gave his attention back to the pretty people in colorful magazine photos. Television stars posing with movie stars at a charity event in Malibu, each subspecies seeking something from the other.

Klosterman said, "I feel like a coward."

Hastings looked up from a photo of Jennifer Lopez's tight bottom. He shook his head.

Hastings said, "Why?"

"I just didn't think I'd feel so afraid."

"Well, you thought you were dying. I'd've been scared too."

"I don't think you would've."

"Yeah, I would've." Hastings stood up. "Listen," he said, "you need to get over these am-I-a-pussy issues. No one thinks that. You hear me?"

"Yeah, I hear you."

"You want to talk to a counselor?"

"Fuck, no."

Hastings hesitated. He wanted to leave and felt ashamed for it. But he wondered if he was embarrassing the man, hanging around. He said, "You want to watch television?"

Klosterman smiled and shook his head.

"George, get out of here."

Hastings took the elevator to the hospital lobby. Walked past a night janitor mopping the floor and out to the parking lot. Once outside, he could hear the sounds of traffic on I-64 nearby, a sound that gave him some respite from the gloom. He liked the city. He still remembered coming to St. Louis for the first time, seeing the arena that was close to Barnes Hospital that was then called the "Checkerdome" and thinking it was the biggest sale barn he had ever seen. He'd been a farmboy then, waiting for the *Midnight Cowboy* theme music to cue up as he walked city streets, wanting to go where the weather suits my *clo-oh-othes*. But the feeling of being an outsider soon passed. People from home thought it strange that he adapted so quickly to it, but he did.

He walked to a chocolate brown 1987

Jaguar XJ6. It was his police unit, the product of a seizure made pursuant to the RICO Act, which the Department had given to his homicide division. The previous owner had replaced the British six-cylinder engine with a Corvette V8. It was a fast car and it made a beautiful burble even when it idled.

Hastings had just unlocked it when his cell phone rang.

He answered it and said, "Yeah?"

"George. It's Karen."

Karen Brady, his captain and supervisor.

"Hey, what's up?"

"Have you heard?"

"Heard what?"

"Two county deputies were shot to death on Manchester Road. Machine-gunned."

If she had just said "shot," perhaps it wouldn't have stopped him so. It happened every couple of years or so; shots fired, officer down. But she hadn't just said "shot"; she'd said "machine-gunned." It suggested, perhaps irrationally, something worse. A societal breakdown, when they were using machine guns. Perhaps too deliberate, too savage.

Hastings said, "Jesus Christ. When?"

"Within the past thirty minutes."

"Is it our district?"

"It's close enough for the chief," she said. "Bobby Cain is already there."

Hastings said, "Why?"

"I don't know. He said the chief called him . . . George, I don't know."

"Ohfff—" George bit off the word before saying it aloud. He liked Karen, but past experiences had taught him that he could not entirely trust her. Certainly not to the degree that he was comfortable telling her what he thought of Bobby Cain. Hastings said, "Don't you think he should have cleared that with me first?"

"Yeah, maybe. But he said the chief of detectives advised him of it and . . ." She trailed off. Hastings realized she had not even spoken to the chief of detectives about it, but she would not question Bobby Cain because she was aware of his influence and she was afraid of him. Afraid of a twenty-six-year-old punk two ranks below her. Jesus.

Hastings said, "So you want me out there?"

"Yes."

"Okay," he said. "Tell me where it is."

She told him and he said he'd get in touch with her later. Karen said, "Well, tomorrow will be all right."

And Hastings thought, well, yeah, for you,

you lazy shit. But again he kept his mouth shut.

He started the car and let the engine idle as he dialed a number.

"H'lo."

"Howard. It's George. There's been a murder. Two murders, two . . . St. Louis County deputies machine-gunned."

"What?"

"Yeah. I think it may be out of city limits, near Rock Hill maybe. But Karen's sending us in. I need you there."

Detective Howard Rhodes said, "Okay. Where is it?"

"The intersection of Manchester and Bryant Place. That's Place, not Avenue. Close to Somerset Lumber."

"Got it."

"Hey," Hastings said, "do me a favor and call Murph. I'll need both of you."

"Done."

Hastings clicked off, dialed another number. He put the Jag into gear and drove to where the parking lot exited onto Kingshighway. He felt relief when he heard the man's voice.

"Bailey."

"Jeff, it's George Hastings. Listen, I need you."

"Is it about the two deputies?"

41

"Yeah."

"Yeah, I just saw it on television. God." Jeff Bailey said, "You've been assigned?"

"Yeah. About two minutes ago. County or even Glenwood PD may have a photographer there already, though I doubt it. Even if they do, we got to make sure there's no gaps. Can you make it?"

"Sure."

"Good. It's Manchester and Bryant Place. Got that?"

"Manchester and Bryant Place. Yeah."

Hastings clicked off that call. Two conscientious detectives and a good crime scene photographer would be meeting him there. He relaxed, a little.

FOUR

A minute later Hastings was driving eighty mph down I-64 with the blue light on his dashboard flashing the traffic away in front of him and Karen Brady was forgotten. God, two cops machine-gunned. Gang-bangers, bank robbers . . . how did it happen? Forest Park whisked behind him as he drove farther west, then got off the exit ramp onto Brentwood Avenue and took it south to Manchester Road, drove farther west until he saw the scene.

He didn't need Karen's directions. The scene was lit up like a night game. Ambulances, a fire engine, camera crews, media trucks with tree-sized light stands for the news correspondents along with at least a dozen patrol cars from metro and county. A large crowd of people, which was not unusual for a murder. But much more than that. Hastings parked the Jag and moved closer. It was then that he realized another distinction between this situation and a typical homicide: the sight of police officers visibly shaken. Crying. Crying because two brothers were slain. And not just by a couple of bangers with Saturday night specials, but machine-gunned. It was as Hastings thought earlier: deliberate, savage . . . something more than a violation of law . . . a rule had been broken.

Hastings presented his police identification and threaded his way through the crowd until he got close enough to see the victims.

And when he did, he was pretty shaken himself. Two county deputies, in uniform, bloody and ragged and undignified in their lifelessness. He found himself choking back a gulp of horror. The cop in him reacted without thought.

"Oh, God," he said, quietly. "Motherfuckers. You rotten motherfuckers."

FIVE

The top-ranking patrol sergeant at the crime scene filled Hastings in before his detectives showed up.

A couple was driving back from the movies when they saw the flashing lights of the sheriff's patrol car and what they thought were a couple of people lying down next to it. They circled back and saw that the men on the ground were police officers. Then they got real scared and called 911. They stayed in their car and left it running because two dead police officers frightened them. Stayed in their car until two other patrol units came and determined that whoever had done the killing was gone. Then they came and gave statements.

The patrol sergeant said, "They felt bad for staying in their car, but I told them they shouldn't. It's a goddamn frightening thing, Lieutenant, seeing two police officers shot to death."

Hastings said, "I know." He put his hand to his mouth for a moment, then took it off. He said, "Did you keep the witnesses here?"

"Of course, Lieutenant."

"Okay. Have the spouses been notified?"

"Yeah. The county sheriff notified them. The young one, Childers, he wasn't married. Hummel was."

"You knew Hummel?"

The sergeant did not swallow, but there was a pause. "Not that well, Lieutenant, but yeah, I knew him. He was a good man. A joker."

"Jesus, I'm sorry."

The patrol sergeant made an effort and kept his voice low and controlled. "Awful," he said.

Murph and Rhodes got there about twenty minutes later. They signed the crime sign-in sheet.

Detective Howard Rhodes was a big, tall man in his early thirties. Hastings did not know him that well because he had only been on his squad for a few months. He was the only black detective on their team and though he was conscious of it he certainly never spoke of it. So far, he had shown the makings of a good detective.

Murph the Surf, the other detective, had

replaced detective Marvin Tate after Marvin got shot by a doctor wanted for murder. Hastings later caught the doctor and arrested him for the attempt to kill Detective Tate as well as for two other murders, one of them committed twenty years earlier. Tate had survived the shooting and had made a good recovery. He sued the doctor for assault and battery in civil court and got a judgment against him for half a million dollars; it was not often that shooters were worth suing, but the doctor had money. After healing, Marvin Tate decided that he no longer wanted to be a police officer. It was an awkward scene when he came to Hastings and told him he was going to become something called a financial planner. Awkward because he felt guilty for quitting and ashamed for being afraid and Hastings felt guilty for being relieved. Because even before the shooting, Hastings had thought that Marvin was not cut out to be a detective. Maybe not even cut out to be a police officer. So they spoke to each other like mutually unhappy spouses wanting to end the marriage without telling the other just why. The detectives took him out to lunch on his last day and when it was done everyone felt the lifting of a burden of guilt and quiet betrayal.

Tim Murphy, in contrast, fit right in. He was in his late thirties and was of a build and size that was almost slight. But he had that air of fearlessness and menace about him that non-Irish cops tend to envy. In another time and place, the English Black and Tans would have placed a bounty on him, dead or alive, though preferably dead. He was a self-assured man who wore sports coats with knit ties that had gone out of fashion during Reagan's second term. Hastings liked him.

Murph and Rhodes greeted Hastings with a nod and "George" respectively and looked at the bodies of the dead policemen. Murph's face twisted in a way that Hastings had never seen before.

Murph said, "Can't we cover them up?"

Hastings shook his head. "No. They have to be left as they are until the MEs get here. You know that."

Rhodes looked away as if he were afraid Murph would start weeping and would need some privacy. It was a human gesture and Hastings noted it.

Murph said, "Who fucking does this?"

"I don't know," Hastings said. "But we've been assigned to it, so I need you to pull yourself together." He looked directly at the older detective. "Okay?"

Murph nodded.

Rhodes said, "You want us to canvass the neighborhood?"

"Yeah," Hastings said. "Take opposite sides of the street and work your way down the block. Then do the block after that. If you have to wake people up, wake them up."

The men nodded and left.

Hastings did not tell them not to talk to any reporters because he knew they were professionals and they already knew better.

Hastings looked across the yellow tape to where a rudimentary command center had been made, outside of the crime scene because the two should never be in the same place. There he saw Chief Mark Grassino, Assistant Chief Fenton Murray, the official department media spokesman Aaron Pressler, and Sergeant Bobby Cain standing in a circle talking.

Right away, Hastings was pissed off. Cain was a sergeant detective under Hastings's command and the place he should have been was next to Hastings asking what he should do next. But no, he was in a conversation bouquet with the Men of Power, nodding affirmations to the brass and standing with his hands in his pockets like he was Bobby fucking Kennedy, the little shithead. Cain came from a wealthy, influential fam-

49

ily. His father was a well-connected attorney, the sort people go to when they're considering running for city council or something similar. As a local kingmaker, Dad could have secured Bobby something simple, like superintendent of public works, but Bobby wanted to be a police officer. And this decision was something of a mystery to the rank-and-file police officers. Some believed that Bobby was using the Department to groom himself for higher office. Perhaps mayor or, years down the road, governor. In any event, they resented him for it. They resented his apparent lack of shame in using his father's name and power to move up the chain of command. George Hastings was not the only policeman who wished Cain would hurry up and finish his apprenticeship and leave them all the fuck alone.

Now, as if on cue to further aggravate the situation, Cain happened to look over and see Hastings looking at him. Cain put his hand up and, using his fingers, gestured for Hastings to come over there.

Hastings had to steady himself and suppress a fair amount of rage. Oh, boy, he thought, someone's going to get his fingers snapped off and shoved up his ass.

Hastings stared back at Cain and then

very deliberately shook his head and then crooked a finger to Cain. No, homey, you come over here. He felt better when he saw Bobby Cain's expression change before he said something to the chiefs and walked over to the primary crime scene. It let some steam off, but not much.

Bobby Cain said, "Hey, George. Uh, the chief wanted to give a statement to the media."

Hastings said, "Okay."

Hastings let a silence fall between them. There was the background murmur of people talking, reporters asking questions, technicians setting up camera shots, police officers swearing and crying while others crossed themselves.

Cain realized Hastings was not going to say anything else. So he said, "Well, I mean, what have we got?"

Hastings said, "Well, let me ask you something: did you get here before I did?"

"Uh, yeah, I guess."

Hastings lifted his hands in a gesture that said, well then?

Cain said, "Well, I was waiting for you to get here and then the chief came and he wanted to know what was going on."

It was a lame rationalization, Hastings thought. But two police officers were dead and Hastings decided not to put any more energy into putting Cain in his place. He thought about giving Cain a short summary of what little he knew to take back to the chief, but he didn't trust Cain. Cain was just the sort to consciously or unconsciously screw it up and have the chief tell the media something completely foreign to Hastings.

Hastings said, "I'll talk to him." He put a hand on Cain's shoulder because he could see that the young sergeant intended to come with him. "I need you to stay here. Talk with the patrol sergeant. He's got all the uniformed officers' statements. Review them immediately and then report to me what you find out."

There was a look on Cain's face as if he were considering it, but before Hastings could say anything, Cain had turned and walked toward the patrol sergeant as ordered.

Hastings's previous contact with Chief Grassino had been limited to a handshake at a fraternal order of police (FOP) Christmas dinner. Mark Grassino was not from St. Louis. Most of his police career had been with the Atlanta police department, where he had been assistant police chief. The city had brought him in and made him chief with the hope that he would improve race relations in the community. No noticeable improvement was made thereafter, but at least people didn't really talk about it anymore. Hastings did not really know the man and had not formed any reason to trust or distrust him.

Chief Grassino shook Hastings's hand and said, "George"; obviously someone had reminded him of Hastings's first name.

"Chief," Hastings said, "I really don't have anything much at this stage. The Pathfinder was stolen yesterday from Florissant. It's machine-gun fire, by the pattern against the vehicle. Nine millimeter slugs, probably from a MAC-10 or an Uzi. It could be that they stopped the driver and the driver got out and hit them with a burst. But I doubt that happened. The positioning of the bodies, I think the shooter would have to have been standing" — Hastings pointed — "there. Or sitting in a car."

The chief said, "A drive-by."

"Maybe."

"On police officers."

Hastings hesitated. "Yes," he said. "Keep in mind, I haven't seen any ballistics report, but unless the driver managed to hide a machine gun beneath his coat or something and then get the police officers between the

Pathfinder and him . . . it's just not likely that happened."

Chief Grassino said, "Are you suggesting that this was set up?"

"Well, a lot of things are possible. But yes, a setup is a reasonable possibility." Hastings looked out at the media trucks. "Respectfully, sir, I would ask that you not tell that to the press."

"You think that would cause some sort of panic?"

"Yes, sir, I do. If people think these men were killed by a random crackhead, that's one thing. If they think it was, well, political . . . that is, if they were targeted *because* they were policemen, well, that scares people."

The chief said, "It scares me too, Lieutenant."

Six

Hastings left the crime scene around 3:00 A.M. and drove home. He lived in a two-bedroom condominium in St. Louis Hills. The condo was on Nottingham Avenue across the street from a park that covered two city blocks. It was a quaint, parochial neighborhood with a vaguely English sensibility. There was a church on each of the four corners of the park, the Catholic one being closest to Hastings's home. Lot of families in the neighborhood. Amy went to school at St. Gabriel's just down the street. Before the divorce, Hastings used to walk her there. Now that he had gotten joint custody of Amy, he still did, though it was no longer everyday.

George Hastings was raised in the Presbyterian church, but he had not attended services regularly since he was a teenager. Anne Klosterman, a devout Catholic herself, had once told her husband that

55

George's agnosticism had something to do with his father being a churchgoing louse, but Joe had said father issues probably had little to do with it and that it may have stemmed more from his general distrust of institutions. Which is not at all ironic for some policemen.

Hastings's ex-wife, Eileen, was also a Catholic, in a way that Hastings had never quite figured out. Eileen actually owned paperback copies of the Catechism, Vatican II, Evangelium Vitae, and Chesterton's *Orthodoxy.* She could tell you the name of a conference that took place in 1930 wherein the Anglican Church formally split with the Vatican over the issue of birth control. She could explain in detail why she thought Cornwell's book *Hitler's Pope* was "a lot of shit." And it was Eileen who filed for divorce and, within three months, married a lawyer she was working for who was about as religious as Ted Turner.

Eileen had given birth to Amy out of wedlock five years before she met Hastings. Amy's biological father was a man who styled himself an artist and left for California before the delivery. He had never attempted to support the child. Eileen had lived with her parents in Kirkwood and finished college. Hastings met her at a party, fell in love with her, and married her. He adopted Amy a year later. No one doubted that he adored Eileen. She was not popular with his friends and certainly not with other cops' wives. But to him she was clever, charming, stylish, and almost too beautiful. He soon discovered, though, that when it came to Amy, he felt he had won some sort of lottery. Until she became part of his life, he had not been aware of how much he could enjoy being a father. Perhaps because of this, he had hesitated to raise the subject of having more children in the early years of his marriage to Eileen. But as time went on, he did raise the subject with increasing frequency.

But Eileen Hastings was not interested in having any more children and she thought well enough of her husband to be candid about it. She had never misled him on that score.

"I'm too self-absorbed to be a parent, George."

"But you're a parent now."

"Not again. I don't want to do it again."

She meant it too. Whatever else could be said about her, she usually meant what she said.

Last year he had found out she was having an affair with her boss. He was mortified and shocked. On top of that, he felt foolish because he had not seen it coming. He, the great detective and leader of men, was unaware. Amy, who was eleven years old at the time, probably sensed what was going on before he did. By the time the divorce proceedings were done, Eileen had ensured that they had joint custody of Amy and had even told Hastings that he would always be Amy's father. He decided that she meant it and was grateful to her. He was not sure he would have survived if he had lost Amy.

Hastings walked up the flight of stairs to his condo, unlocked the door, and let himself in. Closed the door behind him and switched on the lights to an empty home. The condo had a front living room that poured into a dining room, a kitchen, bathroom, and two bedrooms. The living room was sparsely furnished, now that Eileen's knickknacks were gone. Hastings had to admit he liked it better this way. He tossed his keys on a couple of magazines on the coffee table. He read more since the divorce because he had gotten rid of the cable television. Initially, it had been because he feared he would depend on cable like a drug to cope with loneliness, but he soon came to see that it gave him some relief that his daughter was not exposed to HBO or, worse, shows like *The Shield.* Quality television, maybe, but he did not want his twelve-year-old daughter to learn about sex from Kim Cattrall. Such things will bring out the James Dobson in most fathers.

The quiet surrounded him. He was tired. Friday, he thought. Tomorrow is Friday. He would have to pick up Amy at Eileen's and drive her to school. He looked at his watch. If he were lucky, he could get four hours of sleep. If the adrenaline and horror of the dead policemen did not prevent him from closing his eyes and shutting down for a little while.

Ted and Eileen lived in a split-level house in West County. It had five bedrooms and the carpet had been replaced by wood floors. There was a swimming pool in the backyard. Amy said that once, at a party, she had seen Ted jump from the second-story balcony into the pool. She said, "What an idiot." Amy didn't seem to respect Ted very much. She said it was like living with a forty-five-year-old boy. It warmed Hastings to hear these sorts of observations from Amy, and after a time he came to believe that she meant them sincerely and was not just saying them for the sake of cheering him up. Though he would not have minded if that had been her intent.

For his part, Hastings could not really hate Ted Samster. In general, he was not a hater. And the harsh truth was if Ted had not taken Eileen away from him, someone else would have. Eileen simply did not want to be married to him anymore. Sort of like those people who will vote for anyone but Bush. Ted Samster was childish and materialistic, but he was obviously in love with Eileen and there were no signs that he mistreated her or took her for granted.

When Hastings pulled the Jaguar up to the house, Amy was standing out front. She was alone. Hastings felt a pang. He said to himself, what did you expect? That Eileen would be standing out there in her bathrobe — the black and white one he liked to see her in — waiting to greet him and ask, whatcha been up to? Again, he felt foolish. The woman stomps on your fingers as you're hanging off the cliff and you tell yourself, well, she's not stomping as hard as she could be.

Amy got in the Jaguar. They greeted each other and Hastings drove away.

Hastings said, "Do we have time to stop for coffee?"

"Sure," she said.

Sitting at the table at the Clayton Starbucks, a to-go cup sat in front of Hastings, a small bottle of orange juice in front of the girl, her bookbag next to her feet. Pretty morning people came in and out, an old New Order song coming out of the speakers at a respectful decibel. They had about fifteen minutes, at most, to savor there before he took her to school and went to work.

Amy said, "How old were you when you first drank coffee?"

"I don't know," Hastings said. "Maybe a couple of years older than you."

"Did you like it? Then, I mean."

"I don't think so. I started drinking it more when I was in college, to help stay awake in the morning. Then I began to like it."

"Then it's sort of like a drug, isn't it?"

Hastings smiled. "No, it's not a drug."

Amy said, "I saw this movie at Hailey's house the other night. It was black and white. It was just a bunch of people drinking coffee and smoking cigarettes."

"Yeah? Did you understand it?"

"No. One of the parts had Meg and Jack White in it; that's why we rented it."

"Who are they?"

"They're musicians." She shrugged, like it was not worth explaining to him. She said, "Another part had Bill Murray in it. I mean, you know who he is."

Hastings thought of *Stripes.*

"Sure," he said.

"He was drinking coffee straight from the pot. I guess it was supposed to be funny, but I didn't get it."

"He used to be very funny."

"When you were little?"

"Yeah," Hastings said. "When I was little."

An attractive woman in her thirties walked past them and gave Hastings a quick smile. It was the sort of thing that happened once in a while; he no longer wore a wedding band and a man with his little girl does not seem to present a threat. He half smiled back, and resisted the urge to turn and look at the lady's backside. Amy didn't miss much.

Even when he behaved.

She said, "Dad?"

"Yeah, honey?"

"Do you think you'll want to ever get married again?"

"I don't know. Maybe."

"It's okay, you know. If you want to."

"Is it," he said, deadpan. "Can I marry Julia Roberts?" He said it because he and

Amy had recently watched a PBS special together where the star had gone to Mongolia and lived with a family of nomads. No makeup or script, and she was still quite a charmer. Though Hastings believed what had truly enamored him was when she played a coldhearted bitch on a *Law and Order* episode. He had some issues.

Amy Hastings rolled her eyes.

"She's married already."

In the car, Amy said, "Mom is saying she wants to be a lawyer now."

Oh, sweet Jesus, Hastings thought.

But he said, "Really? You mean she's going to go to law school?"

Amy shook her head. She had seen her mother go through a series of failed career attempts. "Who knows?"

"Well," Hastings said, "maybe it will work out."

Amy looked over at him like he was nuts.

He smiled, shrugged, and gestured. "Maybe it will."

They got to the school and Amy said, "Oh, I forgot to ask earlier. Is it all right if Jen comes over tonight?"

"Yeah. As long as it doesn't interfere with dinner. What I mean is, I'm cooking tonight. If you have a friend over, we don't automatically order a pizza. We eat what I cook. Okay?"

"Okay." She kissed him on the cheek. "Bye."

He watched her walk to the school and become absorbed into the mass of uniformed children. You really can't complain, he thought. You really can't.

He was driving east on 64, downtown in view now with the St. Louis Arch looming beyond, when his cell phone rang. It was a number he did not recognize but he answered it anyway, keeping one hand on the wheel. Reckless driving habit, though most cops did it.

"Hastings."

"Lieutenant?"

"Yeah. Lieutenant Hastings. Who is this?"

"This is Justin Elliott, Lieutenant, narcotics."

"Oh, hey. What's up?" Hastings had met him before at a training seminar, but they hadn't said much to each other. The narcs sat at one table and the homicide dicks sat at another, tribes within a tribe.

Elliott said, "I understand you're heading the investigation on Hummel."

"Yeah, both of them."

"Okay," Elliott said. "We need to talk to you."

64

"All right. What is it?"

"Can you meet with us?"

It irritated Hastings, dodging the question. "I suppose," he said. "You guys are on the fourth floor, right."

"No, not at the PD. There's a bar in Fenton, Duke's. It's where the second shift from the Chrysler plant goes after work. You know it?"

"Fenton? That's a forty-minute drive."

"Yeah, I know," the narc said. "Can you do it? We've got a lead. In fact, I think we've got your case solved."

Well ain't that sweet, Hastings thought.

Elliott said, "You know Chester Gibbs, assistant U.S. attorney?"

"I know who he is."

"It'll just be me and him. Can you come alone?"

"Yeah. Okay."

"We'll see you there at ten thirty."

The guy clicked off and Hastings clicked off and dropped the cell phone on the passenger seat. Hastings sighed and took the exit ramp off the highway by the Purina dog food building. Narcotics. In love with a sense of mystery. Hastings remembered a guy in college who was studying aerospace engineering and working part-time for Mc-Donnell Douglas; this was during the de-

65

fense buildup of the eighties. The guy, who was all of twenty at the time, had a habit of telling people he was working on a "black project" at "Mack Doug" and when people would ask him what it was, he would say, "Can't tell you. Secret stuff." Earnest young fool, letting people know he was important. Yeah, you better put your dark glasses on in case Brezhnev is watching. Hastings imagined he had probably helped design some sort of clamp.

Narcs could be like that. Shrouding themselves in mystery and intrigue as they nabbed a series of mid-level dope dealers and forced them to become informants on the bigger dealers and so on and so forth, forever and ever and ever and ever. Hastings himself had mixed feelings about the war on drugs. He wondered if arresting scores of people did any good. Yet he believed that even marijuana use should remain illegal as long-term use did its damage to the spirit. He didn't pretend to know the answer and he didn't have the energy to argue with people who cried hypocrisy and pointed out the damaging effects of whiskey, cigarettes, and over-prescribed Prozac. He believed everybody needed at least a little hypocrisy just to get through the day.

He made a series of turns and got back

on the interstate to head west, out of town. Once he was in steady traffic, he called the station.

Stacy, their secretary, answered.

"Homicide."

"It's George. Let me talk to Murph."

Murph came on and said, "George?"

"Murph, I got a lead. I'll be in around noon."

"Yeah? What is it?"

"Secret stuff."

"What?"

"No, I'm kidding. It may not be anything. I'll tell you when I get back."

SEVEN

Duke's was an ugly, empty little place run by an anvil-faced man who had come from South Philly. The carpet was rough and stained and there was a smell of pickles and hamburger grease and smoke. UAW signs and a picture of labor leaders, including George Meany. But it didn't need to be pretty. In fact, being pleasant-looking would probably have been bad for business. Men and women coming off eight- and ten-hour shifts of doing the same thing over and over would want beers and whiskey in a place that didn't feel too good for them.

Hastings saw the black man wave at him when he walked in. Elliott. There was a white guy with him who looked a little like Dennis Miller from his *Saturday Night Live* days, but with glasses. The guy had an intense look on his face, the face of a man who doesn't want to relax. When he shook Hastings's hand, he introduced himself as

68

Chester Gibbs.

Justin Elliott was tall and slim, in his early forties. He wore expensive cowboy boots, jeans, and a black leather jacket. Handsome fellow. He shook Hastings's hand after Gibbs had done the same, though it was apparent that he would not have otherwise.

The three of them took a booth. Hastings ordered a cup of coffee. Elliott lit a cigarette and pulled a red plastic ashtray toward him.

Gibbs said, "Hummel was undercover."

Hastings waited a moment, looking between the white lawyer and the black cop. Two very different looking men, color aside, but they seemed to share a common seriousness and purpose.

Hastings said, "You mean in narcotics?"

Elliott said, "Yeah."

Hastings said, "But he was in uniform."

"No," Gibbs said. "We're not talking about the night he was killed. Before that, he was undercover. Long-term. Deep. For about —" He turned to the cop for an assist.

"Fourteen months," Elliott said.

"Fourteen months," Gibbs repeated, in case Hastings hadn't been listening. Gibbs said, "He was on a joint task force with DEA and SLPD. We wanted to bust a meth-lab ring run by Steve Treats. You know him?"

"I know of him," Hastings said.

"He was one of the big ones," Gibbs said. "Ran most of the crank labs in South County. White trash guy. But smart, very smart. So we borrowed Hummel from the county sheriffs and sent him in. He was brilliant. A natural."

Elliott said, "When it began, only four people were in the loop. Me, Chester, Chris, and my captain."

"Roger Bejma?" Hastings said.

"Yeah," Elliott said. "Like Chester said, Chris was a natural. In shorts and a ball cap, *I* didn't recognize him. He made buys, got active, got close to Treats. They became friends. Good friends, according to Chris. When Chris testified against him at the end, Treats couldn't believe it. He was sure that Chris was just another dealer turned informant because no cop could have fooled him. He was too smart for that."

"Even at trial," Gibbs said, "the look on Treats's face when Chris testified against him, it was like he was seeing his brother wear a dress."

Hastings said, "You convict him?"

"Yeah. Eighteen to twenty. Treats is in Marion now."

Hastings leaned back against the red padding of the booth. Midmorning gray light came in through the front window. Waylon and Willie and the boys on the jukebox, singing we've been so busy keeping up with the Joneses, the volume set low at this hour so you could hear I-44 traffic in the distance, east to Illinois or west to Rolla and beyond.

Hastings said, "So you think Treats had Hummel killed?"

Elliott tapped embers into the ashtray. He said, "It makes sense, doesn't it?"

"Yeah," Hastings said. "But what about the young cop that was with him?"

Elliott said, "Wrong place, wrong time."

Hastings said, "Yeah, but to put a hit out on a cop . . ."

Elliott said, "You doubt that he did it?"

"I didn't say that."

Elliott said, "Steve Treats is a piece of shit. He's killed before. Rival dealers, but nothing we could ever hang on him. I know what you're thinking, detective. You're thinking this ain't Colombia or Sicily and crooks don't put out hits on police officers. But do not doubt for one minute that Treats is capable of that. He's got eighteen years to spend in prison. Not much to do and a lot of time to think about vengeance."

Hastings said, "I'm not discarding it, Elliott. It's a lead and I'll work it. All right?"

Lieutenant Elliott stared at Hastings for a moment. Hastings let the stare bounce off his forehead and then said, "Why did he go back to patrol?"

Elliott said, "What?"

"Why did Hummel go back to uniform patrol?"

Elliott said, "You ever work undercover?"

"No."

Elliott nodded a *yeah, that's what I thought* and Hastings fought the urge to tell the guy to calm down and put his dick back in his pants because they were both on the same side. He told himself that the narcotics officer had lost someone he knew and liked and maybe deserved the benefit of the doubt. Homicide detectives had a reputation for being snobs who resented the proles telling them their business. There was some truth in this generalization and Justin Elliott probably knew it. Hastings said it again. "No, I never worked undercover." Telling him he won the point so they could move on.

Elliott was quiet for a moment, shifting his mood and posture out of a defensive position. Finally, he said, "Well, if you do it you'd know that you get burned out

72

quickly. You live on doper time, tweaker's hours. They don't start the day until nine or ten o'clock at night; go to bed at seven or eight A.M. And you gotta move when they move because if it's going down, it's going down now. You don't get to make appointments, schedule lunches. There's no structure to the life. And half of the buys don't pan out. Everybody lies. Everybody's a player. Informants who are dealers double dealing cops and other dealers. Try living like that for fourteen months. Chris almost got divorced." Elliott leaned back in his seat. "I guess it doesn't matter anymore."

Hastings said, "So he wanted to go back to patrol?"

Gibbs said, "He wanted to go back to patrol about three months after he started the job. But he said he made a commitment to the job, that he would stay until we got Treats."

And who filled the void left by Treats? Hastings wondered. Probably a thousand applicants. He could ask these guys, but it would offend them and it wasn't his place anyway.

"Okay," Hastings said. "Can you give me your file on Treats?"

Gibbs said, "Anything you need."

"You bring him down," Elliott said. Hastings didn't respond to the order.

EIGHT

Rex Reed's voice was coming out of the radio. Not the sound system that was set in the bar; not the jukebox, but a little Sony radio that Kate had on the rail behind the bar so she could listen to it during the slow hours. Rex Reed was on a talk show guesting with Roger Ebert and it was supposed to be some sort of watershed event; Reed saying nasty things about Jennifer Aniston — "*Rumor Has It* Aniston stinks" — and so forth, Ebert responding that she was actually a very talented comedienne . . . a fop and a movie nerd talking about the girl as if they knew her from high school.

Kate listened to bits and pieces of it, wondering if the gay guy was a permanent replacement for the critic who had died a few years earlier. She thought that might be okay; being gay wasn't his fault and the things he was saying were kind of funny even when they were mean.

She was wiping the bar when the telephone rang. She turned down the radio before she picked it up.

Answering the phone, she said, "McGill's."

"Let me to talk to Jack, please."

"Hold on," Kate said.

She was an attractive woman. On the low side of her thirties, tall, ruddy cheeked, and firm-bodied. She wore her red hair in a ponytail and rarely put on makeup. Jeans and a green T-shirt tucked in at the waist, flattering her form. It was early, between ten and eleven in the morning, and the bar was quiet and clean.

Kate Regan was co-manager of McGill's, a pub in the Bridgeport/Canaryville neighborhood of south Chicago. The bar was in the 11th Ward, approximately ten blocks from the Nativity of Our Lord Catholic Church, where they had Mayor Daley's funeral in 1976. Kate had vague memories of that day, holding her mother's hand as they stood outside the church with the rest of the neighborhood. Kate's mother said the man had built Chicago and that was the main thing to remember.

Kate called out for her husband, twice, before he came out of the back room.

Jack Regan was a big man. He did not

exercise and he still smoked a pack a day, but his appetite was modest and he had not gotten a stomach in middle age. In his mid-forties now, he had streaks of gray in his thick black hair. Black Irish, wearing black slacks and a white collar shirt with the cuffs rolled, more handsome now than when Kate had fallen in love with him. At least, that's what Kate thought.

Kate said, "You got a call."

Jack Regan did not ask who it was. He never asked and neither did she.

Regan picked up the receiver.

"Yeah."

The man on the telephone said, "Can you meet me today?"

It took Regan a couple of moments to place the voice. Alan. Alan Mansell. The lawyer.

Regan said, "We got lunch coming up. Can you wait till two?"

Two meant four. Mansell understood this.

"Two will be fine," Mansell said.

Regan drove his green 1972 Buick Skylark north on Lakeshore Drive and peeled off at the Lincoln Park exit. He parked then walked down the path past sailboats and yachts drydocked and wrapped up for the winter. A few weeks shy of Thanksgiving and the harsh cold wind already coming off the lake, whipping against his cheeks and neck. Regan kept his hands in the pockets of his navy blue pea coat. He had left his gloves at the bar.

He came to a light blue BMW 745Li and stopped to look at it. A man inside, behind the wheel.

Regan walked up, looked in the window, then opened the passenger door and got in.

Alan Mansell said, "Cold out, huh?"

"Yeah," Regan said.

"They say you get used to it," Alan said, "But I've lived here all my life and I sure as hell haven't. I need to move."

Alan Mansell looked like a lawyer. Balding, slight of build, glasses. He wore a tailored suit and an Italian silk tie, a black cashmere overcoat and leather gloves. Lawyer's uniform, which he wore comfortably. He was partners with Lewis Dushane. Neither Alan nor Lewis was Italian, but the local media called them "Mafia lawyers" all the same.

Regan said, "Where would you move?"

"I don't know. Arizona, maybe Miami."

Regan looked around him. "You got a new car," he said.

"Yeah," Alan said, "What do you think?"

"It's all right." Regan had never bought a

new car in his life. He was not drawn to flashy things.

"Yeah, I traded the Jag in for it. It drives better, but it's got this goddamn i-drive thing. Had to have my son teach me how to use it."

"Hmmm." Regan knew less about modern technology than Alan Mansell had forgotten. His own vehicle had the stock AM radio, which was good enough for him.

Mansell realized the man was not going to say anything else about the car or its doodads. He said, "How you been?"

"I've been good," Regan said. "What's up?" It had been almost a year since he'd seen the lawyer.

Alan said, "Zans wants you to help him."

Zans was the nickname for John Zanatelli. He had been arrested and charged with racketeering and conspiracy to commit racketeering. The judge had denied bail and Zans was in county jail awaiting trial.

"All right. Something new?"

"Yeah," Alan said, "you could say that. We got tapes in discovery. Tapes from the prosecution. Like over a hundred of em'. Lewis and I listened to them, but a lot of it's Italian guys and we couldn't understand *what* the fuck they're talking about. We had a set of copies made for Zans and he listened to them too." Alan said, "He understood them better than we did. Anyway. You ever heard of this listening device called a roving bug?"

"No."

"What it is, it's a portable microphone. Sits on the end of a sort of stick or boom. You point it at the people you want to hear and it picks them up. Sometimes clearly, sometimes not so clearly. The feds, they say all these tapes were obtained through legal process; that they had warrants and authorizations from a judge before they used their microphones. They're only supposed to use the roving bugs if they don't have enough information on where and when the suspects are meeting. The thing is though, feds lie to judges. They say they don't know where or when, so they can use the roving bug as much as they want. *Maj*or violation of the Fourth Amendment. Well, that's lawyer talk. The point is, if we could prove that these tapes were obtained wrongfully using the roving bug, if we could prove that the feds misled the judge, we could get the tapes suppressed and kept out of trial. Basically, take away their case."

Regan said, "Okay." He didn't see what this had to do with him. But he imagined the lawyer would get to it. If Zans had sent him.

"Well," Alan said. "On one of the tapes, Zans heard voices, real low, in the background. Two guys talking. And they're not Italian. They're not the guys that are supposed to be bein' taped. They're feds, whispering to each other. See, the feds were whispering to each other while they held the roving bug. Well, Zans played that tape over and over because he heard something that he thought was very important."

"Important to his defense?"

"No," Alan said. "Important to him."

They sat in the car quietly. Traffic went north and south on Lakeshore Drive in front of them, the gray lake and sky lay flat beyond.

Regan said, "Why is that?"

"Because Zans heard one fed say to another, 'Dillon was right.' " Alan paused, said, "Do you understand now?"

Regan said, "You mean Mike Dillon?"

"Yeah."

"Mike Dillon was working for the feds?"

"That's what Zans thinks. And that's all that matters."

Jack Regan smiled. Alan was a diplomat. He was not going to say that Mike Dillon was a rat, working for the FBI. That's what

Zans thinks. Very cautious, very clever.

"How about you, Alan," Regan said. "What do you think?"

Alan stirred uncomfortably in his seat. "It doesn't look good," he said.

"Okay," Regan said. "Zans thinks Dillon ratted him out."

"That's right."

"Well, it would explain some things, wouldn't it. Mike disappearing, Zans's arrest. Danny's arrest. Yeah . . . it would explain a lot."

The U.S. attorney used something called the kingpin statute of Illinois along with a lot of federal codes to snag Zans and some other guys. Most of them Italians, some of them Irish. The local media and some law enforcement referred to them as "dinosaurs," bit players trying to relive Mafia nostalgia. But even the U.S. attorney had said it wasn't as simple as that. The counts filed by the U.S. attorney had asserted that John Zanatelli had been operating a "continuing criminal enterprise." And he was right about that. The enterprise had many employees, principals, and agents. Some of them lawyers like Alan Mansell and some of them freelance assassins like Jack Regan.

Though Jack Regan never thought of himself as an assassin. He didn't think of killing in such high-minded concepts. He had quit counting how many times he had done it over the years. Some years, as many as five. Some years, none at all. He did count the money, though. He always counted the money.

Alan Mansell regarded Regan now.

"You believe it?" Alan said.

"I don't have trouble believing it," Regan said.

"But you know Dillon."

Better than you, Regan thought. Mike Dillon — Irish Mafia chief and federal rat. But anyone with sense enough to discard the blarney would know that Mike Dillon was capable of anything. Dillon, who spoke of Ireland like it was a mystical, magical homeland but had never once been there; who lived with his mother until she died, but had made widows of other mothers; who talked about keeping drugs out of the south side, but took weekly protection fees from every dope dealer south of Thirty-first Street. Jack Regan was no moralist, but he hated blarney.

"Right," Regan said. "Zans want him clipped?"

Alan Mansell hesitated. He knew Jack Regan's business and he knew that Zans had insisted that they use Regan. He got right to it, and maybe that was a good thing. Still, the man's attitude chilled the blood.

After a moment, Alan said, "Yes. That's what John, what Zans wants."

"Okay," Regan said. "You know where he is?"

"Dillon?"

"Yeah."

"No, I don't know."

Regan knew Alan's partner had once represented Mike Dillon. Regan turned slightly in his seat.

"You sure?" Regan said.

"Yeah," Alan said, getting his meaning. "I'm sure."

"I don't judge, Alan. I'm just asking."

"I know what you're thinking," Alan said. "Yeah, we've represented Dillon before. But that was years ago. Zans is our guy now."

Regan sighed, hid a smile. "Bloody mercenaries."

Alan smiled. "You in?"

"How much?" Regan said.

"Hundred."

"Hundred?" Regan said, "For Dillon?"

"That's a lot of money."

"Not for Mike Dillon. He's a lot of things, but he ain't dumb. He's probably got body-guards. It ain't the same thing as a millionaire in a parking lot."

"Well —"

"Well, what? I get clipped, my wife's got to run our place alone. We eat up a hundred in overhead in less than a year."

"We'd make sure she'd get taken care of."

Regan stifled a laugh.

"Would you now? Come on, Alan. I've heard that shit before. Remember Timmy Frears?"

"That's —"

"They told him to keep his mouth shut and they'd take care of his wife and kids. Well, he did and his family went on welfare. Humiliating. Things like that make a man sitting in prison wonder who his friends are. And that's a man who was alive. You gonna tell me you'd treat his family better if he were dead?"

"Okay," Alan said, "you made your point. What do you want?"

"Well," Regan said, "I'm not lookin' to retire on it. Just fair treatment, that's all. I'll do it for two."

"Two hundred?"

"Yeah. Half now, half when it's done."

Alan Mansell made a face.

"Come on, Alan. We both know Zans clears fifty a week with his operation. He can spare two hundred and more."

"Okay," Alan said. He took an envelope

out of his coat and handed it to Regan. "There's fifty in there. We'll get you another fifty tomorrow. You get the other hundred when it's done."

Jack Regan put the envelope in his pocket. "Good seeing you, Alan." He got out of the BMW and walked back to the Buick.

NINE

There was a plaque on the wall behind Karen Brady's desk that said WHEN YOU *ASSUME* YOU MAKE AN ASS OUT OF U AND ME. It had been there for two years and Hastings wondered what it would take to get her to take it down. Joe Klosterman had once suggested that they break into her office after shift and replace it with a sign that said WHEN YOU PUT DATED LAME-ASS SLOGANS ON A WALL, YOU MAKE ASSHOLES OUT OF ALL US. For a while, Hastings actually feared that Joe would do it.

He was in her office now because she had called him in right after he got back from Fenton and asked to "assess the case." Hastings told her about the lead from narcotics.

"That's great," she said.

Hastings had a concern. He debated bringing it up because he did not want to show her disrespect.

87

"Well," he said, "it's just a lead."

Karen frowned. "What?"

"I mean," Hastings said, "I don't think we should tell the assistant chief just yet. Certainly not the department spokesman."

"Is that what you thought I was going to do?"

Yes, Hastings thought.

"Oh, no," Hastings said. "I mean, no — I didn't think you were going to suggest that."

"What's your concern?"

"My concern is, it's just a lead." Hastings said, "Frankly, my concern is with these guys."

"You mean Lieutenant Elliott?" Karen said. "Why? Is it a race thing?"

Jesus Christ, Hastings thought.

"No," he said. "It has nothing to do with — no. Elliott's okay. I think Gibbs is okay too. The thing is, they feel responsible. They knew Hummel. They liked him. And they hate Treats. They *want* it to be Treats, is what I'm saying."

"So you don't think Treats did it?"

Hastings mentally sighed.

Hastings had worked for Karen Brady for two years. He did not dislike her. She was ambitious to be sure, but there was little about her that was ugly or cold. She was, at root, a nerd who wanted to both belong and be respected, and this is a difficult mix for a person in a position of leadership. She had never been more than a mediocre detective. She was inoffensive and unimaginative and she was not especially strong. In the upsidedown world that is often police administration, these traits helped her float, more or less unnoticed, to the rank of captain.

"No," Hastings said. "There's good reason to think he did do it. We've got a motive. And I want to check him out. But it's just a lead now. That's all it is. What I'm worried about is word leaking out that the case has been solved. Because it hasn't."

"How would that happen?"

Hastings thought of one Bobby Cain. And he worried about Karen too. Ambitious people wanting credit for a closed case, moving quickly, screwing it up and making fools of good people.

"It can happen," Hastings said. "And if it leads to nothing, we've given the victims' families a false hope."

"I'm not going to lie to my superiors."

"Karen, I'm not asking you to. They ask, we answer. People are scared and they want answers. I understand that. But . . . well, you see where I'm coming from?"

"Yeah, yeah," she said. Her tone dismissive now; she didn't like it when you made sense. "Where is Treats?"

"He's in Marion. I'll go out there tomorrow."

"Alone?"

"No. I'll take Cain with me."

Karen Brady looked at him, confused. But she didn't ask why and he didn't tell.

TEN

Dillon liked the Stouffer's prepackaged macaroni baked in the oven because if you heated it in the microwave, you couldn't get the cheese to brown on top. Sharon had cooked it in the microwave once, thinking he wouldn't know the difference, but he had, and he threw it against the wall and made her clean it up. Sharon Dunphy had wiped the sauce and noodles off the wall and floor and told herself that Mike had never hit her. Never slapped her or cuffed her on the head. She just had to remember to do things properly.

Dillon had said to her once, "What do I ask from you? Huh? Come on, tell me. What do I ask of you?"

What he asked of her was that she have a decent meal on the table every night at six o'clock. Not much, he said, considering that he was paying for the food as well as her mortgage. In fact, he didn't even press for sex. Once every couple of weeks or so, he would take her to bed. Which she didn't mind so much. Mike Dillon was older than she was, but he was not a mean-spirited lover. No rough stuff. And he looked good naked for a man of his age. There were times when Sharon wondered if Mike even enjoyed doing it. She wondered if he was making love to her not because he wanted to, but to prevent her from thinking he was a fag or something. They said it happened to some men when they served long prison sentences. Get used to things men shouldn't get used to. He had told her he spent most of his twenties and early thirties in Leavenworth.

Tonight, she had cooked the macaroni in the oven and she didn't take it out until a brown crust had formed on top. She took it out of the oven and transferred the steaming pile from its plastic dish to a dinner plate. She took asparagus from the stovetop and put it next to the macaroni. Then she put a dinner roll on the side. One roll, not two. Mike was always careful about keeping dinner portions small. Fifty years old and no stomach on him.

Mike Dillon put the *St. Louis Post-Dispatch* down as Sharon put his plate in front of him. He said, "Where're the kids?"

Sharon said, "Matt's at band practice. Lee's at her friend's."

Dillon frowned. "They should be here for dinner," he said.

They weren't his kids. But he was funny about these things. The family should eat together, he said, even if the family was not his. Sharon shrugged, hoping he would leave it alone for now, and he did. At another time, he might have lost his temper and told her she was a shitty mom, maybe broken something and walked out. But tonight he let it go. You could never tell what Mike was going to do.

At thirty-two, Sharon Dunphy was eighteen years younger than Mike Dillon. She was an attractive woman with blond hair she usually wore in a ponytail. In makeup and nice clothes, she would have been very pretty. Prettier still without a look of fear and dread wearing down her expression.

The father of her children, Matt Senior, had worked for one of Dillon's associates years ago. But he got caught driving a truckload of stolen cigarettes near Kansas City and had to go away for a seven-year stretch. Before that, Matt had introduced her to Dillon like he was the pope or something. Dillon had made a point of remembering her when he showed up in St.

Louis a couple of years ago — this time to stay, apparently. Dillon said it was a shame about Matt getting caught, but he was here now and he wanted to take care of her and the kids. He had his own place, but he liked to have dinner at their house at least three times a week.

This night, he finished his dinner and put his plate in the kitchen sink. Rinsed off the gunk and put it in the dishwasher. Sharon remained at the table. Dillon put his windbreaker on and kissed her on the top of her head.

"I'll see you later," he said.

She looked at the window and watched him get into his car and drive away. It gave her some relief. But only some because he would be back. He always came back. She sometimes wondered if it would be better if he did hit her. If he did get violent with her. She wondered if that would relieve some of the pressure she felt. Her life had not been one of contentment or happiness or quiet comfort, but until she met Mike, she had never known the burden of feeling so scared. Not just sometimes, but all the time. Even when he was gone, the fear remained. It was constant, overwhelming. It was like a prison. Bad enough before, but now it was beyond bad. Now it was a nightmare. She had learned to control the crying, had learned to be quiet. And sometimes she thought that having to be quiet was the worst of it. Like watching a horror film, but you're not allowed to cry out or scream or even draw breath. You just have to remain silent and hope he doesn't notice. Sit quietly in your own horror movie.

ELEVEN

It was a two-hour drive to Marion, and it didn't take long for Hastings to figure out that he did not want to use that time to foster some sort of friendship with Bobby Cain. Cain talked about work, college, high school, football, the Rams, Mizzou, Coach Woody, his father, his father's law firm, his wife, and other women. He was vulgar when he spoke of women. Holding forth on a previous fiancée who was a runner-up in the Miss Missouri pageant, he said, "I had a good ride on that, lemme tell ya." And so forth. Hastings, who had seen a number of things inexplicable and gross, wondered how this man had ever gotten a woman to marry him. He wondered if the man had close friends and, if so, did they talk this way also? They had taken Hastings's car, so Hastings was driving and could not pretend to take a nap to get the guy to be quiet. He made a note to ask Cain to drive on the way back. If he didn't kill him before then.

Hastings told himself that it was necessary to bring Cain along. He was a sergeant detective under his supervision and there was nothing he could do about that. Work was a series of compromises and he couldn't very well ask Karen to transfer Cain out because Cain got on his nerves. Cain would have to screw up first. And, considering Cain's influence in the Department, that screwup would have to be more than substantial. Besides, it was too risky to leave Cain behind because Cain may not have been able to resist the urge to call the assistant chief or his dad or his uncle and tell them about the Treats lead and how they had just broken this case wide fuckin' open. Keep your friends close, Don Corleone, and your incompetent careerists closer.

About halfway there, Cain said, "I guess you don't talk much in the morning." Wounded, for God's sake.

"No," Hastings said. "Sorry. I'm kind of tired."

"Thinking about the case?"

"Yes."

"So, is it true you played baseball for SLU?"

"Yes."

"So what was that like?"

Oh, God, Hastings thought. He said, "It was okay."

"I guess it's hard to make a living at that."

"Yeah, I imagine it is."

Hastings passed a truck, put some distance in front of it, then slipped the Jaguar back into the right lane. The windshield wipers were set on intermittent, knocking off the drops left by a light rain.

Cain said, "So, you're kinda young for a homicide lieutenant."

Hastings looked over at the young sergeant. Men with more experience and time on the street were nowhere near Bobby Cain's rank. Hastings said, "Not really."

"Oh, no; I mean, that's impressive. I mean, how does that happen?"

"How does what happen?" Hastings said it mildly.

"How did you become a lieutenant before turning forty?"

"I took an exam and got promoted."

"Yeah, okay. That's cool, that's cool."

There was a silence. Hastings debated turning on the radio, wondering if the forced laughter of an FM morning show would be preferable to this conversation. He decided it would not be.

Hastings said, "Bobby?"

"Yes."

"Did you review the officers' reports?"

"Yes. I did it the night you told me to."

"What did you find out?"

"Neighbors heard the gunfire. Some of them thought it was kids setting off firecrackers. Probably old people, hearing aids on the blink. One witness saw a dark car drive by. Nothing more than that. No tags. Not even a good description of a vehicle."

"How many people in the car?"

"Nobody saw."

"Well, that's not good. What about the Pathfinder?"

"Stolen that afternoon."

"Owner report it?"

"Uh, yeah. As a matter of fact they did." Cain removed a notepad from his inside pocket and flipped through pages till he found what he wanted. Hastings was almost impressed. "Yeah, here it is. Reported stolen at 1440 hours. No identifiable prints."

"But the deputies," Hastings said, "did they know that?"

"Did they know it was stolen?"

"Yes."

"Well, no, it appears they didn't. I mean, they didn't call it in."

"Right. But did they call in the tag when they pulled the vehicle over?"

"No, they didn't."

Hastings said, "Why not?"

"Why not?"

"Yeah. Why didn't the deputies call it in? Right after they pulled the Pathfinder over, why didn't they follow standard patrol procedure and call in the tag number?"

Cain was uneasy now. "I don't know."

Hastings shook his head. "No, you gotta help me here. We talk these things out; that's how it works. Why didn't they call it in?"

Cain hesitated and looked at Hastings, wondering if they could go back to the part where he talked shit and Hastings got bored.

"Come on, Bobby. We speak freely here."

After a moment, Cain said, "Okay. Well — I mean, I wasn't there, so —"

"So what?"

"Well, so maybe they fucked up."

Well, Hastings thought, whatever Cain was, he was not totally brainless. And at that moment, at least Cain was aware of his youth and inexperience and the danger of second-guessing cops who died in the line of duty.

Hastings said, "Yeah, they might have." He didn't enjoy saying it, but it was the most reasonable explanation.

Cain seemed to feel better after that.

Steve Treats had the boyish good looks of a

surfer. Blond hair, good teeth. He wore the light blue prison fatigues casually and comfortably. In the interview room, he sat leaned back in his chair, his hands in his pockets, legs stretched, his feet crossed. Hastings sat in a chair at a right angle to Treats, his body also relaxed and his legs crossed, the two men doing a dance, striking poses and staking out territory. Blocking and acting, as wolves do. Necessary tasks for detectives conducting interviews and suspects wanting to prove how clever they are.

Bobby Cain was young and had not yet learned these things. He started out in another chair, restless, wanting to strike.

Treats said, "So somebody whacked Chris. Well, anyone can tell you I didn't do it." Treats gestured to the walls.

Cain said, "You could have had it done."

Treats glanced at the younger policeman, as if he just now noticed him. More wolf behavior. "Think so, junior?" he said. "Who am I gonna find that will whack two cops?"

Cain said, "Money can buy anything."

"Not security," Treats said. "One thing I've learned in this wonderful life is that if someone wants you dead, you're gonna die. They may not get you today, but they'll get you tomorrow. You're marked, you're marked. Something else I know: you kill a cop, the cops kill you. I know the rules."

Hastings said, "That's not what we've got in mind."

Treats said, "Yeah? You know what happened in Soulard four years ago, don't you. That guy shot a cop in the alleyway and they made Swiss fuckin' cheese out of him. *After* he surrendered. *After* he put his gun down. Tell me if any of those cops got charged with murder."

"No," Hastings said, affecting mock curiosity, "I don't believe they did."

Treats said, "You ever hear about Murray Flint? He jumped bail on a grand theft auto charge. The cops came to get him, and he ran onto the roof of his building. Tall building on the North Side. Well, Murray, he happens to kick one of those guys in the nuts. They get mad and, as they put it, there was a 'scuffle' and poor Murray fell off the building. But what really happened is they just plain got pissed. So they grabbed his feet and his hands" — Treats mimed it — "one, two, *three!* And threw his ass off."

Hastings smiled. "Come on, Steve, cut the jailhouse gossip. That happened about fifteen years ago."

"I know what I know."

"You know what you heard in here.

They're all innocent in here."

"Those cops that threw that fucker off the roof, were they innocent?"

"It's an old wives' tale, Steve. Why don't you get to the point?"

"All right, Lieutenant," Treats said. "The point is, I wouldn't go in for killing cops. I'm getting out of here before I turn fifty. Every day I think about that. Every day. It's the only thing that keeps me going. I'm not going to fuck that up to get even with a piece a shit rat fuck like Chris Hummel."

Cain leaned forward. "You better watch your mouth," he said.

"Ah, fuck you. What are you going to do to me, junior?"

"We can make things hard for you," Cain said. "You want to find out, you keep pushing it."

Treats said, "Junior, I can lawyer up and end this interview right now and you know it. You are here because I let you come." Treats looked at Hastings as he said it. Then he spoke to Hastings directly. "You're barking up the wrong tree."

Hastings said, "What do you mean?"

Treats said, "Hummel was dirty, man. He was taking money from dealers all over South County. Selling cases. It ain't hard to figure out, even for a cop."

Hastings said in a flat tone, "Is that right?"

"Yeah, that's right. My guess is, he finally got too greedy, asked for too much. There's your homicide case."

Hastings regarded Treats for a moment. Then he said, "That's quite a theory you have there, Steve."

"It's the truth, man."

Hastings said, "You have proof of this?"

"The proof is out there, if you're willing to see it."

Cain stood up. "Oh what is this," he said, "the fucking *X Files*? Out there if we want to see it? You're just talking shit."

Hastings said, "Okay, Steve, tell me this: did this . . . smart bomb of yours ever come up at your trial?"

Hastings saw the man's body language shift. Just for a moment, but he saw it. After a moment, Treats shrugged and said, "No." Like it was no big deal.

"I see," Hastings said. "Why not?"

"Ahhh, my fuckin' lawyer. I told him to use it, but he wanted to go another route."

In addition to innocent men, the prisons were also filled with guys who had dipshit lawyers. Hastings shook his head at the man.

"But you check it out," Treats said, "if you got the balls to do it. You'll see what I'm talking about."

"We're gonna check *you* out, fuckhead," Cain said. "Count on it."

Steve Treats turned and looked at Cain again, deciding to acknowledge him with a blank expression. Then he turned back to Hastings.

Treats said, "We're done talking."

TWELVE

It was around eleven thirty in the morning and there were four people in the bar. Couple of guys in a corner booth drinking Old Style, the bartender, and Stanley Redd drinking an Amstel Light. The girl behind the bar was a twenty-four-year-old chippie with a stud in her lower lip and a white stomach bulging out of her tight white T-shirt. She looked good to Stanley Redd, who was in his mid-thirties, balding, and with bad skin. He had the *Chicago Reader* in front of him and his eyes went from the football scores to the girl's chest like a dotted line from a comic book character. He thought he had a chance with the girl.

At eleven thirty-seven, Regan came in and took the barstool next to Stanley's.

The girl walked over and gave Regan a smile that depressed Stanley Redd, not least of all because Regan was older than he was.

Regan said, "Cup of coffee, with cream.

And get this fellah another beer."

Stanley Redd said, "Thanks, guy." And felt a bit of a stone in his heart. He hoped the guy was a fag or something, not because he liked men, but because it would explain a complete stranger sitting next to him when there were a dozen other barstools the man could have taken.

Regan looked up at the television behind the bar. Fat white people being interviewed by Maury Povich. The trouble with young people today, Regan thought, is they'll watch anything on television. Like old ladies.

The bartender brought back coffee in a white cup on a white saucer with the spoon on the side. Regan liked that. He preferred coffee in cups, with a spoon to stir rather than a wooden stick. She set another bottle of Amstel in front of Stanley Redd.

Regan said, "Taking the day off?"

Stanley Redd said, "Uh, yeah."

"Cold out," Regan said.

"What?"

Regan turned to look at him. "I said, it's cold out."

"Yeah, it's getting cold."

"Good to be in a nice, warm place like this. Know what I mean."

"Yeah."

"It'll snow soon. We'll have to drive through all that snow. That Range Rover you drive, has it got four-wheel drive?"

Jesus. He's not a homo, Stan thought. His heartbeat quickened.

Regan said, "I mean, you can't drive that little convertible of yours in the snow, can you?"

Stanley Redd looked at the fresh bottle of beer in front of him, the sides sweating. He managed to force a smile as he said, "Yeah, well that's cute." He started to get off the stool.

Regan put a hand on his wrist.

"Where're you going?"

Stanley Redd said, "What do you care?"

"Stanley, sit down, finish your beer. We can handle this like gentlemen or we can go put you in a back room for three of the worst days of your life. We'll get what we need either way."

Jack Regan spoke quietly to Stanley Redd. He did not use the word "torture" or explain what it is they did for three days. In his experience, people's imaginations worked better for him. Particularly for people who did business with criminals. Most of them understood.

Regan said, "We know where you live, where your parents live." Regan gestured to the bar around them, "We know where you go. You can leave town, go on a vacation, but you can't leave home forever." Regan spoke in a gentle tone, not unlike that of a priest, letting the confessor know he would feel a whole lot better getting that sin out of him. "Okay?"

Regan kept his hand on the man's wrist and he could feel it quivering now.

Stanley said, "Who are you?"

Regan shook his head. The question was not relevant. He said, "I know about you, Stan. I know who your friends are. Believe it or not, I'm the best friend you have. You've got a situation now and I'm going to help you out of it. You understand?"

"No, I don't."

"You and your friend Max, if you want to call him a friend, you hired Jimmy Rizza to torch your nightclub three years ago. Relax . . . I'm not here to blackmail you. I'm just letting you know that I know. Okay? I know a lot of things."

"Man, that was —"

Regan lifted his hand, gesturing for silence. He knew the guy was wondering now how Regan knew him. They had never met before. But Stanley Redd had never quite gotten a handle on mob culture. It was not a thing you could just dip your toe into, then walk off.

Stanley Redd and Max Collins were pals — a sort of Ben Affleck/Matt Damon combo who had been moderately successful entrepreneurs. Nightclubs, start-ups, that sort of thing. Quick money, cocaine, strippers. They *were* smart, book smart, but they had been lucky too. But like a lot of young types who get rich, they tended to discount the luck factor.

Moreover, they wanted to be cool. Having money wasn't good enough. They wanted to be hip. They wanted to be street. It was when they got into the nightclub business that they hooked up with Jimmy Rizza and his little brother. Stanley and Max were *attracted* to the Rizzas. Not in a physical way, per se. But because they were dangerous, funny, raucous, lively. They were interesting. The way they talked, the stories they told, so . . . *entertaining.* Stanley said they should have their own show. He liked introducing them to women, and enjoyed later having to put rational fears at rest by saying, "No, he's all right. He's just from a different world than you and I." Showing them that *he* wasn't afraid because he understood them, you see. It was neat being part of that world, maybe persuading yourself that you were only near it and not in it.

But Regan knew it didn't work that way. Once you let guys like Jimmy Rizza in the door, they stayed. And the favors that Jimmy Rizza did for you usually became common knowledge in the criminal enterprise. It was its own little community and secrets were often shared.

Regan said, "Stan? I just need to know one thing: where is Max going to be to-night?"

"What?"

Regan squeezed Stan's wrist, watched the man wince as he fought the urge to cry out. Regan knew it was not hurting him that much, that the tears came more from fear of what else Regan would do. Again, imagination.

"Stan? Don't test my patience, all right? You don't want to do that. Where is Max Collins going to be tonight?"

Stanley Redd pictured himself sitting on a stool in a back room, naked and bloody, bruised and broken and humiliated. It was working on him and they both knew it.

"He's got a girl. Jesus, uh, he's got a girl. He keeps her in an apartment —"

"Where?"

"Marina City. The Towers."

"Which one?"

"What?"

"Which apartment?"

"I don't know. Christ, I swear I don't know."

"You've been there, haven't you?"

"Yes, but — uh, wait. It's on the forty-second floor. That's all I remember. The south tower."

"What's the girl's name?"

"Stacy. Stacy Racine. He goes there usually between six and eight in the evening. That's all I know, I swear."

Regan looked into the man's eyes for a moment. Then he released his grip.

"Okay, Stan. I hope you're right."

Regan stood up and placed a five dollar bill on the bar before walking out.

Stanley Redd, hearing his heart thrum in his ears, hoped he was right too.

THIRTEEN

They walked out of the penitentiary and past a crowd of activists holding signs that said FREE VICTOR. Got in the car and left the smell of the correctional system behind them.

It was still drizzling.

Hastings looked over at Cain and said, "You can't do that."

"Can't do what?" Cain said.

"You can't let people like Steve Treats rattle you. He called you 'junior.' Okay, so what? We got black police officers who get called nigger. You think they like that? When I was in patrol, some turd once said my mother sucked a mean cock." Hastings shrugged. "It doesn't mean anything, Bobby. The guy doesn't even know you."

"We shouldn't have to take that shit."

Hastings shook his head. He was not comfortable giving lectures. But he was getting irritated now. "Don't take this the wrong way, Bobby, but are you sure you want to do this?"

"Do what?"

"*This*. Police work. You got a college degree. You could go to law school, work in your father's firm. You'd make more money and no one would call you names there." Not to his face, anyway, Hastings thought. "I mean, why would you choose to do this?"

"Why would you choose to?"

"I'm not you."

"Not gonna tell me, huh? That's cool." Cain said, "Well, I don't want to be a fucking lawyer. I'd die of boredom."

"This work can be boring too."

"I don't think so. Still," he said, "don't you ever think of, you know, getting even?"

"With who?"

"With Treats? People like him. Don't you ever think about that?"

"No," Hastings said, and meant it. "Getting even isn't part of it. Treats is a loser. He'll die in prison or he'll die of old age. It makes no difference to me. You start thinking about getting even with people like him, you're gonna ulcer a hole right through your stomach."

"Christ, didn't it bother you?"

"Didn't what bother me?"

"What he said about Hummel? You're

okay with it?"

"No, I'm not okay with it. He called a brother a crook. I'm not okay with that."

Cain said, "I don't understand; now you're saying it does bother you?"

Shit, Hastings thought. Of course it bothered him. It bothered him anytime a cop was accused of being dirty. It bothered him more if it was true. Because if it was even remotely true it reflected on every police officer in the city. Him, Klosterman, even Bobby dickhead Cain. That was why it was necessary to investigate every dumbass complaint that came down the pike. Hastings suddenly felt tired. He prayed there was nothing to it. If there were, it would make everyone unhappy. The brass, the patrol officers, the sheriff's office and, of course, Hummel's poor wife. He pictured the nightmare headline: CROOKED COP HAD IT COMING.

He remembered the patrol sergeant and Murph fighting back tears at the crime scene. He remembered his own rage and despair upon seeing the two young officers slain like animals. Young men who would never feel the melancholy of middle age, never reach the age where they would talk about their days of young turkdom with the cop's mixture of self-deprecation and pride.

Members of his own tribe, his own team. How would it be to add the taint of corruption to their murders? Fucking right it bothered him.

Hastings said, "That's not what we were talking about."

"Okay," Cain said. "What Treats said, you going to put that in your report?"

"Yes." Hastings looked at the younger cop, corruption on Hastings's mind now. He knew what Cain was suggesting: that the report could become exculpatory evidence, maybe even help the person that killed the police officers and that maybe it would be better for everyone if they just forgot what they had been told. But what had happened at Marion had happened and there could be no lying about it.

"You do the same," Hastings said. "Understand?"

"Yes, sir," Cain said. He stared straight ahead when he said it, letting Hastings know what he thought of him.

They drove in silence, Cain saying no more about his father or sports or women that he had given a good ride. He did not talk about anything.

Still, Hastings felt better to get it out. He didn't have to worry anymore about this coming back on him. He believed the Bobby

Cains of this world were just the sort who would blame a false report on someone else. *The lieutenant told me it was okay.* Those concerns didn't go away when you advanced in rank; they got worse, in fact.

FOURTEEN

When he returned to his office, he found Justin Elliott sitting at his desk.

"Hey," Elliott said, "What'd you find out?" Elliott did not seem at all embarrassed.

My, my. Hastings thought of the dumbass who had lectured Bobby Cain on keeping your cool. He silently counted to five so he wouldn't pitch Justin Elliott out the window. He was aware of Cain watching him.

Hastings said, "Get the fuck out of my chair."

"Hey, man," Elliott said, "take it easy. We're all on the same side."

Hastings said nothing. After a moment, Elliott got out and moved around the desk to the front. Hastings remained standing.

Elliott said, "You need to mellow out."

Hastings said nothing. He moved behind his desk and took his seat back. Then he said, "What do you want?"

"You didn't call me," Elliott said. "I wanted to know what you found out."

Hastings said, "Listen, I'm glad you want to help. But let's get something straight right now: I report to Captain Brady, not you. You got a problem with that, you file a complaint."

"Goddamn, what is wrong with you?"

"This is my desk. My investigation. Accept it."

"Oh, I'm sorry," Elliott said. "I forgot this was homicide. Shit doesn't stink around here."

"I'm not checking in with you, Elliott. I'm sorry you lost a friend, but I'm not checking in with you. I'm not going to seek your okay on things."

"I'm not here to take credit, detective. You want all the glory, you can have it. I just want justice."

Christ, Hastings thought and almost smiled to himself. Again with the glory. He had had a good run a couple of years ago. Caught a serial killer and hooked a group of home invaders. Good police work that he was proud of. And there were newspaper articles about it. He never had his photograph in the newspaper or appeared on television, but more than one officer had called him "glory boy." Partly he was annoyed, partly he was flattered.

Hastings looked at Elliott for a moment. Then he said, "You want some coffee?"

Elliott looked back at Hastings for something else. Finally, he said, "Yeah, I'd like some coffee."

"Bobby, will you get us some coffee? Then let's all sit here and talk about this thing."

Bobby Cain's heart had been in his mouth. He thought he was going to see the two policemen start swinging at each other. He had never seen Lieutenant Hastings fired up. And then like that, it was over, and the black guy was taking a seat in front of Hastings's desk.

Cain came back with two coffees and set them on Hastings's desk. Hastings gestured for him to take a seat too.

Hastings said, "Treats told us Hummel was dirty."

"What?"

"He said Hummel was selling cases. Taking money from dealers."

"That's a fucking lie."

"I'm just telling you what he said."

"You believe it?"

Hastings said, "I've got no reason to believe it. No proof of it. Yet. But I have to check it out."

"What the hell you mean, *yet?*"

"I don't *want* to believe any of it. But I have to check it out."

Elliott leaned back in his seat. "So check it out," he said.

"What do *you* say?"

"I say it's bullshit."

"Why?"

"Because if Chris Hummel were taking money, I would have known about it."

"Any way he could have done it and you didn't know?"

"Lieutenant, I've got informants around this city you've never heard of. If Chris had been taking money, I would know." Elliott said, "Here I thought you were smart; do you believe everything a convict tells you?" Elliott looked over at Cain after he said that, attempting to mutiny the other cop against Hastings.

"Oh for Christ's sake, Elliott, don't hand me that shit," Hastings said. "You think Treats is just gonna tell *me* this? He wants to dirty Hummel's name, he's gonna tell everyone he can. You think I want to help Treats with that, you're insane."

"What *do* you want?"

"I want to clear it up. There's a difference between doing that and hiding it. Now, you want to help me do that or not?"

A moment passed and then another. Then

Justin Elliott shook his head and said, "How do I help you do that, Hastings? How do I prove he *didn't* take money? It's like proving a negative." Elliott looked at Cain. He said, "You're going to put it in your reports, aren't you?"

Cain's expression answered the question, involuntarily.

Elliott stood up to leave. "I told you Treats was smart," he said, "but you didn't listen. You're letting him play you."

"No," Hastings said, "I think you are."

"Fuck you," Elliott said and walked out.

When he was gone, Cain picked up the coffee cup he had left. There was still coffee left in it. He set it next to the coffee pot.

Cain said, "Wow. Do you know that guy?"

"I know of him."

"What a jackass."

"He's got a good reputation," Hastings said.

"He acted like you were accusing *him* of something."

"Did it sound like I was?"

"No," Cain said. "No, not to me." Cain relaxed a little. The ugliness had passed and the men had not tried to hit each other or drawn their weapons. He regarded Hastings.

"Do you?" Cain said.

"What?"

"Do you think Elliott's on the take?"

Hastings looked over at Junior Cain. He had picked up on a distinction between showing and thinking.

"I don't think so," Hastings said. "The guy's paranoid. It happens to narcs." Hastings left it at that. But he knew that paranoia was not limited to narcotics work. It happened to detectives and patrol officers too. When he was younger, Hastings had worked under the supervision of a patrol sergeant, Merl Davidson, upon whom he'd foisted superhero status. To the young patrolman Hastings was then, Merl seemed infallible. Brave, smart, wise, tough, and cool. A man born to lead men. And then three years ago, he ran into Merl at an FOP meeting and Merl had become a shell. Questioning the most minute things, unsure, his skin pale, his body language and eye movement fearful and anxious. The same man Hastings had looked up to, now broken. Merl told Hastings about an internal affairs investigation on something that seemed and, indeed, turned out to be inconsequential. Yet Merl kept asking Hastings, "What do you think? What do you think?" Seeking affirmation from the police officer he had once mentored. It made Hastings feel ill. Hastings had heard that

Merl had gone through a nasty divorce, his wife fed up with constant accusations of infidelity that had no basis in reality. No tragedy or death scare had befallen Merl Davidson. A decade and a half of watching and questioning and suspecting had simply taken its toll. Hastings did his best not to judge because he knew it was a hazard of the profession and that no one was immune from it and you were a proud fool if you thought otherwise.

Hastings said, "He did come to me first."

"Elliott?"

"Yeah."

"Okay," Cain said. "But maybe that was for his benefit."

"What do you mean?"

"I mean, sooner or later we'd've found out about Hummel working undercover. So maybe it was in Elliott's interest to, you know, put us onto Treats."

"It's possible," Hastings said. A lot of things were possible. "But it's not likely. It's more likely that Treats wants to start a rumor, piss on Chris Hummel's grave."

"What difference would it make to Treats? Hummel's dead."

Hastings shrugged. "Upset his wife. Embarrass the Department. Look at it from the perspective of an evil man."

124

"So you think Treats did have Hummel killed?"

"I think it's a lead. But the problem is, Treats spoke to us."

"So?"

"So, he's not stupid. He spoke to us without an attorney. That's something dime-bag dealers do. Not a major player like Steve Treats." He said, "Not if he's guilty."

"So you're saying Treats is using us?"

"Well, he succeeded in pissing off one narc already. And he's more or less ruined my day."

"You said earlier, 'Not if he's guilty.' Again, you think Treats had nothing to do with this?"

"I don't know. I think Treats sang hallelujah when he heard Hummel was killed. But I don't know that he had it done."

"Why not?"

"Like I said earlier, if he had, there's no way he would have talked to us. I reviewed his jacket. Not once did he agree to an interview with the federal investigators. No deals. He went to trial."

"Yeah, and he was convicted. Things're different now."

"Okay, they are. But did you hear him ask for anything today? Did you hear him offer to give us anything? Did he ask us to reduce his sentence, make any calls for him?"

"You admire him?"

"Uh, no."

"Sorry." Cain recovered, said, "All right then, what was in it for him?"

"Vengeance."

"Okay. But what about Elliott?"

"What about him?"

"Is he lying to us?"

"I don't think so," Hastings said. "He thinks Treats is evil, and he's right about that. The guy wants to make Hummel's widow suffer. But Elliott *believes* Treats was responsible. But, as you know, you can prove murder without motive. But motive on its own —"

"Is not enough," Cain said. "Yeah, I know."

Rhodes and Murph came in to the squad room. They had spent the morning continuing the canvass of the neighborhood. Hastings asked them how it went.

Murph said, "Nothing substantive. How about you?"

"Treats didn't give us anything. Told us Hummel was taking money."

"Ah," Murph said. "What a shock."

"Yeah, well, I didn't take it so nonchalantly myself. This is going to get out; Treats or his lawyer will make sure of that. I don't think there's anything to it, but we've got to investigate it anyway before it's all over the news."

Rhodes said, "But how do you prove a man's innocence?

"You know," Hastings said, "people keep pointing that out to me." He said to Rhodes, "You busy now?"

"Well, we've got to write our reports."

"Why don't you do that later? I need you to come with me."

FIFTEEN

They rode out west in Rhodes's take home Crown Vic, Rhodes driving as Hastings told him how he came to know Kody Sparks.

Hastings said, "Kody and a buddy of his were at a honky-tonk in South County. Norm's. You ever hear of it?"

"Oh, yeah. Go there all the time."

Hastings shrugged. Okay, Howard Rhodes wasn't partial to Toby Keith or Garth Brooks. But neither was Hastings. And hadn't Willie Nelson once kissed Charley Pride on the mouth in front of a bar load of cowboys? Ah well, leave it alone.

Hastings said, "Well, Kody and his buddy — Reggie was his name — they get in a pissing match with this other turd at the place, his name was Charles Lane — they start throwing fists and the bouncer throws them all out. So they continue the fight outside and then more bouncers come out and tell the guys to get in their trucks and go. So they do and half a mile down the road Charles Lane starts bumping his pickup into the back of Kody's. Now, it's Kody's truck, but he's not driving it, Reggie is. Reggie decides they'll finish it and he stops at Carondelet Park."

Rhodes said, "I heard about this."

"So, if it were left to Kody, they wouldn't have stopped. He doesn't want to fight. He wants to go home or go someplace else. So he told us. So Kody and Reggie get out of their truck and Charles and another guy get out of their truck and I guess Charles Lane and his pal just start getting the shit knocked out of them. Charles Lane and his buddy get back in their truck, Charles gets behind the wheel and runs Reggie over. Killed him. Then took off."

"Killed him?"

"Yeah. Well, it was a fairly easy case. Witnesses from the bar, motive, Lane had a few assault and battery arrests, etc. Charles Lane hires this hotshot lawyer and they wouldn't take any deals from the district attorney's office. None. Could have taken eight years in on a second-degree manslaughter plea. But no, they wouldn't do that. The DA gets pissed, charges Lane with second-degree *murder*. We go to trial and Kody is one of the prosecution's chief witnesses. Well, Kody had about four or five arrests for drug possession, intent to distribute. Crank, mostly. DA couldn't keep it out of evidence, so he admits upfront to the jury that Kody has a record. And we had to more or less babysit the guy during the trial. Buy him a nice suit, you know the drill."

"They convict Lane?"

"Oh, yeah. Lane claimed self-defense, but the jury didn't buy it. Luckily, the victim was pretty clean. That helped." Hastings said, "Kody was a pretty good witness, actually."

"So you kept in touch with Kody?"

"I've talked with him a couple of times. He's still underground and he hears things."

"Still cranking?"

"I don't ask," Hastings said.

Howard Rhodes did not judge. Rare was the detective who did not use an unsavory witness in a criminal trial. He said, "Well, people don't change."

Hastings looked at Rhodes and wondered if he was experienced enough to be forming that opinion. He remembered Klosterman saying the same thing to him. It was around the time Eileen moved out, and Klosterman was trying to suggest, in a diplomatic way, that Hastings shouldn't expect her to come back.

Hastings said, "Turn here."

They pulled up to a gray covered house in Dogtown. There were two county patrol cars in front. A large woman stood on the front porch, yelling at the police officers as they led a short, fat man away in handcuffs. There was an Arab yelling back at her, the officers keeping him back.

"Oh, shit," Hastings said.

Rhodes and Hastings got out of the Ford and approached the officers. They showed their identifications and asked what was up.

A heavyset deputy said, "He was caught shoplifting. You know him?"

Kody Sparks said, "Hi, Lieutenant."

Hastings said, "Hi, Kody." To the deputy he said, "Yeah. I know him. He testified for us in a case once."

The deputy gestured to the Arab. "He owns the corner grocery store. This guy went in, stuffed some donuts into his pockets, and walked out. Mr. Awan asked him to come back and empty his pockets and Kody took off running. Right here."

Hastings said, "You found the donuts on him?"

The deputy seemed to sigh. "Yeah. He never took them out."

Kody's mom yelled, "He didn't steal nothing."

The other deputy: "Ma'am, just stay there. Please."

Rhodes said, "Well, this is bad timing."

The first deputy took Hastings aside and said, "Listen, we have to arrest him. The store owner insisted. It's his neighborhood too."

Hastings said, "I'm not asking you to cover for him."

Kody's mother said, "He's a goddamn liar." She was pointing to the store owner. "They're all goddamn liars."

The second deputy muttered, "Oh, shit."

The first deputy said, "Listen, Lieutenant, we're about to have a fucking racial incident here. Can we clear the area, please?"

"I understand," Hastings said. He walked over to Kody. "Kody, they gotta take you in. I'm sorry. Do you have a lawyer?"

Kody said, "Whoever they give me."

"I'll call Sam Hall. He'll get you a lawyer to O.R. you out. We'll try to do it tonight."

"Thanks, Lieutenant."

"But Kody, I need to talk to you. All right?"

"Sure, Lieutenant."

The deputy put him in the backseat while Rhodes walked over to the store owner and told him that the suspect was being arrested and he needed to leave and that an officer would get a full report from him later. The store owner looked at the black detective warily and Rhodes decided not to notice it. The store owner said, "It's my business. Mine."

"Sir, we understand that. Now please leave. Please."

The store owner glared once more at the detective before walking off.

The patrol cars left, taking Kody Sparks with them. And then Rhodes and Hastings stood awkwardly on the sidewalk as Mrs. Sparks began to cry.

Hastings said, "I'm sorry, Mrs. Sparks. It's a minor charge. He should be home tomorrow."

"He could have just asked me for the money," she said. "I would have given it to him."

"I know you would have," Hastings said. "Listen, I think he'll be home tomorrow."

"You promise?"

"We'll see," Hastings said.

"He's just a boy," she sobbed. "Just a boy."

Later in the car, Rhodes said, "Just a boy. He's thirty if he's a day."

"Oh, Christ," Hastings said. "Give her a break, willya?"

SIXTEEN

When Max Collins's wife found out he was screwing his secretary, she made him fire her. She did not threaten to divorce Max or leave him; she liked his money too much for that. And she knew Max liked his money too and, consequently, would not divorce her. She knew her Max. He had to live with his wife — some of the time — so he fired Stacy Racine and set her up in an apartment. As Max said to a friend, "Hey, anyone can type." A line he'd heard in a movie.

If someone had told a young Max Collins, say, in his college years, that he would one day support a mistress, he would not have believed it. To a chubby, ugly kid with glasses, such a thing seemed so remote as to be impossible. For his older brother, perhaps, who had always done well with women, it would seem not at all unlikely. But Max had been a virgin until his senior year of college. And that event had been embarrassing, to say the least.

Stacy Racine was twenty-three years old. Young and not quite slender with a stud in her belly button and implants Max had paid for. Max Collins, now thirty-nine, was still pudgy, still freckled, still devoid of charm. He wore steel-rimmed glasses and suits cut to hide the fat, but his posture still lacked confidence.

But he was a wizard with numbers. Graduated second in his class at Caltech, then got his MBA at the University of Chicago before working in finance. He made enough money by the time he was thirty to retire comfortably. But he went on and became a venture capitalist. He could support a few Stacy Racines if he were so inclined. But just one was wearing him out.

On this evening, Max called Stacy from his Mercedes G500 SUV ("the big one," he would tell people) to make sure she was in the apartment. Make sure she was alone. One time he had come over to find her with another girl and some kid of about twenty wearing his jeans low on his hips. Clothes were still on but Max did not like the shit-eating grin on that kid's face. After they cleared out, Max said, with a nervous chuckle, "Gee, you guys weren't about to have a threesome, were you? Heh-heh." He was relieved when Stacy denied it and told him he was "sick in the fuckin' head." Max pretended to believe her.

Stacy answered the phone.

"Yeah," her tone unenthusiastic, insolent.

"Hey, baby," Max said.

"Hey, Max. Did you get the boots?"

He had ordered her a pair of boots from Marshall Field's because when they had been there earlier the store didn't have her size. Max agreed to pick them up later.

"Yeah, yeah. I got them."

Max pictured an airbrushed version of Stacy, sitting on a milking stool in a barn, legs slightly apart, wearing just the boots. . . . He said, "You gonna model them for me?" Heh-heh.

Stacy said, "Why? You saw me wear them in the store."

Jesus, it was hard. She never seemed to get his jokes. The *Playboy* photographer looking over at Max now, shrugging his shoulders because the model wasn't cooperating, the photographer telling Max, I can't work with these people.

Max said, "Well, I just thought that . . ." He gave it up. Maybe he had to say it to her in person. He said, "I'm coming into the Towers now. I'll see you in a minute."

In rare lucid moments Max could admit

to himself what Stacy was. Or had become. Still, he wished she could at least humor him once in a while. Okay, so she didn't want to model the boots for him. Couldn't she at least feign interest in the idea? With all that he had given her, all that he had spent on her, would it be so difficult to show a little consideration?

Stacy Racine was the third girl he had ever slept with. The second was his wife. The first was the girl in college who never spoke to him again. That encounter had seemed, well, *short*. And if he hadn't understood that himself, the girl certainly made it clear to him afterward. She apparently mistook him for someone else.

Linda, his wife, was strictly a missionary position, Catholic girl. They were together once every three weeks or so. Linda would not take her top off because she was shy. She remained shy throughout their marriage.

Stacy Racine was anything but shy. For Max, Stacy Racine was a whole new world. She did anything and everything. Some things she wanted Max did not particularly enjoy, but if he didn't comply, she'd call him a fag. Which seemed a little ironic to Max, given her penchant for anal sex. It did not occur to Max that in her own way, Stacy

Racine found sexual intimacy every bit as indecent and unpleasant as his wife did. For Linda Collins, it was dirty. For Stacy Racine, it could only be dirty.

Max drove the Mercedes in ascendant circles up the spiral of the south "corncob" of the Marina Towers. He parked on the eighteenth floor, the vehicle's front looking out to the Chicago River. It was dark now and the city was lit up. A train crossed the river and auto traffic bustled over the Michigan Avenue Bridge. Max got out and closed the door of the Mercedes, heard the sound of the characteristic, satisfying *thunk* that justifies the cost of the vehicle. He felt the chill of night air, coming off the lake and cutting through the open space of the high-rise garage.

"Hello, Max."

Max felt his stomach jump involuntarily. He turned to see Regan standing behind him. A big man, standing in the space between the Mercedes and a Ford van parked next to it. Blocking that space.

Max tried to swallow away the quivering of his chin. He said, "Hey . . . do I know you?"

Regan said, "We met before. At McNamara's. Don't you remember?"

"Uh . . . I don't know."

"Jimmy Rizza introduced us. You remember *him,* don't you?"

"Uh, Jimmy —"

"Rizza," Regan said, staring the man into recollection. He wasn't going anywhere.

"Oh, yeah," Max said. He spoke as if they were at a party, as opposed to a garage ledge eighteen floors up. He forced a smile on his face. "Yeah, I remember now. How you doing?"

Regan didn't answer. He didn't smile either. He said, "You remember what we talked about?"

"Uh, no. No I don't."

"I do. Actually, I didn't say much then. But you and Jimmy, you talked about burning down a nightclub. A nightclub you and Stan owned." Regan said, "You remember that?"

Max was silent for a few moments.

Regan said it again. "I remember it."

"Hey," Max said.

Regan walked in between the vehicles, closing in now, and Max stepped back, looking over his shoulder as he did so, into the void.

Regan said, "You kept in touch with Jimmy after that. Didn't you?"

"No, I did not. I never saw him again."

"Ah, Max. That's not what I heard."

"Well, I don't know what you heard, but —"

"You were losing money in another venture of yours. Another business. And one of your partners talked about reporting you to the SEC." Regan said, "And that fellah disappeared, didn't he?"

"I don't —"

"Convenient for you, huh?"

"I don't know what happened to him."

Regan said, "*You* happened to him, Max. You and Jimmy Rizza. You paid Jimmy to clip him."

"What are you, a cop? There's no proof . . ."

"I'm not a cop, Max. I'm not interested in proof."

Max Collins should have known better then. He had dipped his toe into the criminal underworld, enjoyed associating with the bad boys, had taken a certain pride in it. So he should have known something about them. But he remained a man unaware of his own lack of awareness. Had it been otherwise, he would not have asked Jack Regan this next thing.

Max Collins said, "Hey man, are you wearing a wire?"

Regan stepped forward, quickly, and grabbed Max by the lapels of his camel's hair overcoat, pushing him off balance so that he stumbled and then Max's upper body was out and over the edge of the precipice, feeling the pull of gravity on his shoulders. All Regan would have to do was drop him . . .

Regan said, "You ever even *suggest* I'm a rat again, I'll kill you. Last warning. Understand?"

"Yes, yes," Max cried. "I understand. *Jesus,* please."

"I don't wear wires for nobody. I handle things me own self. Understand?"

"Yes, yes —"

"Where's Jimmy?"

"What?"

"Where is Jimmy?"

"I don't know."

Regan relaxed his hold.

"Jesus! I don't know. He disappeared."

"I know he disappeared, you fucking idiot. But he kept in touch with you. Don't tell me he didn't because I know he did."

"He —"

"You know how I know, Max? You know why you're still alive now? Because I understand Jimmy. When a man like Jimmy does a man like you a 'favor,' he puts it in the book. He comes back and asks you to pay for it and keeps coming back. Right?"

"— right —"

"Now where is he?"

"He left Chicago —"

"And?"

"He left town. Two years ago, he left. You know, when the feds issued warrants for him and Dillon. Somebody tipped them off and they left town."

"Where?"

"I don't know. *Don't!* I don't — I think they're in St. Louis."

"Where in St. Louis?"

"I don't know where. I swear to Christ I don't. I'd tell you if I knew. I just know he has a safety deposit box in St. Louis. I swear that's all I know."

Regan stared into the face of raw terror for a moment, Max's ears shrinking back like an animal's. He pulled Max back from the edge and let him slump against the Mercedes. Max slipped to the ground. He was still crying.

Regan said, "I'm going to assume you're being honest with me. But if there's something you left out, tell me now. Tell me now and I won't be mad. If you don't tell me and I find out later, you'll die." Regan said, "Okay?"

"I've told you everything I know. I swear

on my kids."

Regan left the man on the ground, crying.

SEVENTEEN

The wine hissed and spattered when Hastings poured it into the pan. He stirred it around with the olive oil, onions, garlic, meat, and peppers. He would let it simmer until the alcohol burned off. Then he would add the tomatoes and the paste. It was a recipe Eileen had taught him. She was a good cook when she wanted to be.

The telephone rang.

"Amy," Hastings said. "Get that, will you please?"

A moment later, Amy brought the receiver. "It's someone named Sam Hall. You know him?" At twelve, Amy was good at screening out telemarketers.

"Yeah." Hastings gestured for the phone, wedged it between his head and shoulder.

"Sam?"

"Yeah, George. You page me?"

"Yeah. Listen, I gotta guy got arrested this evening by county deputies on a minor shoplifting charge."

"Okay. You want him bonded out?"

"Yes. I want him out."

It was an unusual request for a police officer. But Sam Hall did not push it. He had been on the force himself years earlier before he left and started a bail bonds business. Hastings imagined he made a lot of money, though he seemed to end up with more cars than he did cash, clients valuing freedom more than their vehicles.

"When?" Sam said.

Hastings said, "Tonight. His mom's upset."

"They all got mothers."

"Just help me, all right?"

"Well, okay. Let me see what I can do. You say he's at county?"

"Yeah. His name is Kody Sparks." Hastings spelled it out.

Sam said, "Okay. You gonna be at this number for a while?"

"Should be here all night."

Sam hung up and Hastings handed the phone back to Amy. Then he asked her to cut the French bread up and put it in the oven.

Amy said, "You want a beer?"

"Yeah."

She got a Heineken out of the refrigerator and popped the top off. She set it next to the stove so he could sip it while he cooked. Then she sat back down at the dinner table with her friend Jennifer, a frequent guest at Amy and George's evenings together. They chatted about kids at school and other things Hastings made no attempt to listen to.

Sam called back after dinner.

"Okay," he said, "I got a lawyer who'll O.R. him out tonight. Her name's Carol McGuire. You know her?"

"Carol McGuire . . . isn't she with the P.D.'s office?"

"She used to be. She went out on her own a few months ago. She doesn't need the business; she's doing it for me." Sam said, "She can meet you at county jail at nine o'clock. She'll want money."

"How much?"

"Two hundred for the trip. Can you handle that?"

"What'll she be wearing?"

"What?"

"Nothing." Hastings said, "Two hundred's okay."

"Listen, don't be mad at her. She's all right. And she's driving out there at night."

"I'm not mad at her. I don't even know her."

"Okay. Well, surely the kid's mom can come up with the two hundred."

Hastings gave Amy the standard instructions before he left: don't unlock the door for anyone, let the answering machine answer telephone calls, and call his cell in case of emergency. He drove the Jag to a bank kiosk and cursed with resignation as he withdrew two hundred in flat, crisp twenties.

He saw a willowy looking woman of about his own age sitting in the waiting area at the county detention center.

Hastings said, "Carol McGuire?"

The woman said she was and stood up to meet him. She gave him a mechanical handshake.

Carol McGuire was pretty without makeup. She wore jeans and a gray sweater under a mackintosh raincoat. Her hair was dark and short and straight.

Hastings said, "Thanks for coming."

She gestured a *never mind* and said, "I've already checked in with them. They're getting him now."

"Great," Hastings said. He reached into his jacket pocket. "I brought your fee."

She looked at him.

"Why are you paying it?" She still wore the wary expression public defenders have around law enforcement officers.

"I don't know," Hastings said. "I really don't. He's helping us on a case."

"What kind of case?"

"That's confidential."

The woman shook her head. "I'm not going to let you talk to him alone," she said.

Hastings said, "It's not up to you. It's up to him." He was getting irritated now. Two hundred dollars poorer and now a lady lawyer was giving him heat. He wished Sam Hall was here to explain why he had sent this woman.

The McGuire woman was still looking at him.

Hastings said, "Ma'am, I need to question him about the murders of the two deputies who were killed the other night. Okay?" Like, happy now?

"That's your case?"

"Yes. I'm in charge of the investigation."

"Is he a suspect?"

"No," Hastings said. "He is not a suspect. You want me to write it down and sign it?"

"All right, calm down." She said, "What do you want to ask him?"

"I'll ask him that."

Hastings walked away from the woman and sat on the bench. It was a calculated move, intended to make her feel insignificant.

But when he took his seat on the bench and looked back at her still standing, he thought he saw the hint of a smile on her face. It surprised him. Willowy and pretty in her way, but no pushover.

Then the hint of smile was gone and she was still looking at him. She said, "I saw it on the news. I'm sorry."

Hastings made a gesture. We're all sorry, aren't we?

The woman said, "You're not mad at me, are you?"

Yeah, she was tough all right. "Yeah," Hastings said. "Furious."

Carol McGuire walked over to a wall and leaned back until her shoulders rested against it. Her face was at a right angle to Hastings and her hands were in her coat pockets. A cool pose, he thought. Yet she didn't seem the sort to pose. Hastings looked at the way her dark hair contrasted with her fair-skinned neck. Was still looking as her head pivoted slowly toward him, busting him. She regarded him, unembarrassed.

Hastings said, "I was trying to remember

if we'd met before." He felt awkward.

"We haven't," she said. "I've seen you at the courthouse before. You always look so serious."

Okay, enough with the patronizing, he thought. "Yeah?" Hastings said. "I hear you're pretty mean yourself."

"Did you." The woman seemed unimpressed.

After a moment, Hastings said, "You quit working for the P.D.?"

"Yes." She wasn't going to say anything else.

Hastings said, "I don't blame you."

The McGuire woman didn't seem to like that comment. She gave him a glance that was mildly hostile, but left it at that.

Hastings felt conscious of himself then. Did all recently divorced men have this sort of trouble communicating with women? The last date he had had was . . . oh, God, eight years ago? Then he thought, why are you thinking in terms of *dates?*

They heard the buzzer sound as the first door unlocked, and they could see people and movement through the small square window of the second door separating them from lockup. The second door buzzed open and out came a deputy escorting Kody Sparks. He was back in street clothes, tired and unwashed; looking like he just got out of jail.

"Hey, Lieutenant," Kody said.

"Hey, Kody," Hastings said. "This is your attorney, Carol McGuire."

Kody was confused. He looked at the woman. He said, "What?"

Hastings said, "She got you released on your own recognizance. Using her bar card."

"Yeah, I know that," Kody said. "But I mean, what's she doing here?"

"Well . . ." Hastings said, looking between the woman and the informant. The woman seemed confused too, and not happy.

"Well," Hastings said again. "Are you hungry, Kody?"

"Oh, hell yeah."

"You want to get something to eat?"

"Yeah, man. If you're buying."

The McGuire woman stepping forward now —

"He's buying all right," the woman said. "Kody, as you attor—"

"Ms. McGuire's going to join us," Hastings said. "Maybe she's hungry too."

The three of them sat in a booth in Irv's, an old eatery off Vandeventer Avenue. It was run-down and the red seats had tears in them. The food was cheap and bad. Night people sitting at the counters and tables. The locals said that Irv's was a dump and it should've been bulldozed into the ground years ago, but there it stood. Kody ordered the "nightmare" platter: chili over eggs cooked sunny-side up. Hastings looked at the dish and remembered a time when he could eat such things. He ordered coffee. Carol McGuire ordered coffee too.

Hastings was tempted to laugh at this scene. Mom and Dad taking Sonny out for dinner. Welcome home, Kody. From jail. It was what Joe Klosterman would call surreal.

Hastings said, "Kody, I need to ask you a few things."

Kody stabbed on the egg yolks with his fork. The yellow bled out into the surrounding chili.

"Okay," Kody said.

"You know Steve Treats?"

"Yeah, I know him."

"You know he's at Marion now."

"Uh-huh."

"You know how he got busted?"

"Sure, I know."

Hastings said, "How?"

"Undercover cop ratted on him."

"So you know about that?"

"Everybody knows about that."

Hastings didn't tell him he'd found out about it yesterday. He said, "You knew about the undercover cop."

"Well, I knew about it after they arrested Steve."

"The cop," Hastings said. "His name was Chris Hummel."

Kody was bent over his plate. "Yeah?" he said.

"You remember him?"

"Yeah, I remember him."

Hastings said, "Did he ever take money?"

"Who?"

"Chris Hummel."

Kody broke off a piece of white Wonder Bread and dipped it in the yellow-brown mixture.

"You mean from Steve?"

Hastings said, "I mean, from any dealer?"

Kody Sparks shrugged. "I never heard that he did."

Hastings was aware of the McGuire woman staring at him, but he forced himself not to look at her. He said, "You telling me the truth, Kody?"

"Yeah." Kody looked up from the meal. "I wouldn't lie to you, George. You and Sergeant Joe been good to me. Where is the sergeant, anyway?"

"He's in the hospital."

"Ahhh. What's wrong?"

"He's fine. He had a little surgery. He'll be all right."

"Well, you tell him I said to get well."

"I will." Hastings said, "So. No word on the street that Hummel was taking money?"

"Nope."

"Kody, let me be clear: if there was, it's okay to tell me."

"I know that, George. There wasn't."

Carol McGuire said, "You offering something, Lieutenant?" Some edge in her voice.

"No, ma'am," Hastings said. To Kody, Hastings said, "What about Steve?"

"He's in jail."

"I know that, Kody. I mean, did Steve ever tell you or anyone you know that Hummel was taking money?"

"Nope."

"Never?"

"Never."

"Lieutenant," Carol McGuire said. "May I speak to you in private?"

"Sure." Hastings said, "Kody, we're going to go outside for a minute. We'll be right back."

Moments later, Hastings and the McGuire woman stood outside against the dirty white front of the food shack. Behind them, interstate traffic rumbled over Vandeventer and Kingshighway, forcing them to speak in voices slightly raised.

The McGuire woman said, "Are you trying to make me a part of this?"

Hastings said, "A part of what?"

"Buying crank dealers dinner?"

Hastings shrugged. "He was hungry."

"That's not the point."

"What is your point?"

"My point is, you're using him to cover up for another cop."

That stopped him. Up till then, he had known, in a way, that she was an adversary. Or was in adversarial position, which maybe wasn't quite the same thing. But he had not expected her to hit him with something like that. He felt it then; anger rising and he wanted to control his tone of voice.

"No," he said. "Goddamn it, that is not true. I did not do that."

"You —"

"Were you too goddamn busy judging me to listen to what was said in there? I told him at least twice *not* to tell me what I wanted to hear. Twice, I told him that. Christ, why do you think I asked you to come along?"

"You had no choice."

"Oh, shit, lady. I could have driven around the block and picked him up after you left.

You'd've been none the wiser. Did you once see me threaten him? Did you once see me ask him to lie?"

"You got him out of jail. You buy him chili and eggs. He's an addict. He'll tell you whatever you want."

Hastings patted his jacket pocket. "It's all on tape, Ms. McGuire. I have done nothing I'm ashamed of. You want to try to twist it into some sort of obstruction conspiracy, you go right ahead. But I've got tape."

It pushed her back on her heels. But only for a moment. She said, "Spare me your sanctimony, detective. I know how you guys work. If the tape helps you, you keep it. If it hurts you, you erase it. Tonight, it happened to help you. And by the way, what do you mean 'twist it'? What are you accusing me of?"

"You're the one doing the accusing. And, worse, you're doing it just to do it. I know your type, madam. You've got issues with cops. They're all dirty as far as you're concerned."

"You don't 'know' me at all. What — do you think I popped open a bottle of champagne when I found out that two police officers had been killed? Two cops whacked. Yippee."

"I don't know. Did you?"

"Oh for God's sake," she said. "Everything's so black and white with you people. I'm not on your enemies list, detective. I'm not on the side of murder."

"Well just who are you representing now? Huh? And don't tell me it's Kody Sparks because we both know this isn't about him." Hastings said, "You accuse me of covering things up. On whose behalf are you doing that? You stand there defending someone we don't even know yet. Someone we haven't caught. Someone who murdered two men."

She stood quietly there in her jeans and raincoat, her cheeks red with cold or anger. She stood there neither ashamed nor afraid. Finally she said, "Well, you seem to have made up your mind about me."

She went back into Irv's, leaving him outside alone.

EIGHTEEN

The door to McGill's opened and two guys came in. One of them took a stool at the bar and the other one stood and leaned against it. They were both in their thirties. The guy sitting on the stool wore a porkpie hat and a gray suit and a tweed overcoat. He was heavy and short and round. People who knew him called him Bacon. The guy standing against the bar wore wool slacks and a black leather jacket. He was taller and thinner. His name was Sean Rizza.

They ordered Miller Lites and asked to see the menu.

Kate Regan brought it to them.

Sean Rizza looked around the place. He saw two guys at the other end of the bar who did not concern him. He saw two other people in one of the high-backed booths across from the bar; a guy leaning forward on the table to talk, a girl sitting with her legs up on the seat and her back against the wall. She was smoking a cigarette.

Kate Regan said, "I recommend the stew tonight. It's very good."

"Yeah?" Bacon said. "Hmmm."

Sean said, "You cook it?"

Kate looked at him briefly. "No," she said. "We have a cook."

"Is he in the kitchen now?"

"Yeah," Kate said. "That's where we generally have our cook."

Bacon smiled. "She's funny."

"Yeah," Sean said. To Kate he said, "Why don't you bring him out here."

Kate Regan said, "Why don't you pay for your beers and leave." She was not going to say anything else.

"She's tough too," Bacon said.

Sean stepped back so she could see him pull the lapel of his jacket back. There was a .357 revolver tucked into the waistband of his pants. He said, "See that? Good. My buddy here's going to go back to the kitchen with you. You'll come back out with the cook and then we'll help you round the customers up. Okay?"

For a moment, Kate didn't say anything. Then she nodded. Bacon followed her to the kitchen. They came back with the cook.

When they got back to the front, Kate saw that the guy with a leather jacket had pulled a black ski mask over his face. She turned and saw that the short one had done the same. The short one pulled a sawed-off shotgun from beneath his coat and directed the customers and the cook into the storeroom. He locked them in there. They took the ski masks off after that.

He came back with three cellular phones that he placed on one of the tables. He said to Sean, "Everyone's got a phone these days."

Sean said to Kate, "Now get back behind the bar. Keep your hands on the bar. We don't see your hands, you're going to die."

Kate took her place behind the bar. She watched as the porkpie sat in the booth opposite the bar and put his shotgun on the table. The leather jacket stayed at the bar with her.

Kate said, "I don't expect him back tonight."

Sean said, "He's coming back, honey. I'm betting your life on it."

She looked at the porkpied man. He was nestled back in the booth with its high backs directly across from her. From where he was sitting he could not be seen from the front door. Or from the back. He was well hidden.

Sean saw movement through the front

window. He said to Kate, "You stay where he can see you."

Sean moved to the front door. A customer got in the foyer before Sean put a hand on his chest.

"We're closed tonight, buddy. Sorry."

"But the sign says —"

"We're closed."

The customer sensed something dangerous about the man. He backed out. Sean moved back to the bar, but this time leaned against the part of it that was close to the door. He looked down the length of the bar at Kate Regan and made sure she had obeyed his instructions. She had; her hands were still on the bar.

Fifteen minutes went by.

In the sixteenth minute, another customer came to the front door. Sean told him the same thing he had told the other one. The guy left.

The doors to the train opened and Regan stepped out and walked past the turnstiles and down the stairs. Night and it was colder now. He used trains more than he used his Buick. Chicago traffic made for miserable driving. The trains were easier, more civilized. And he liked walking afterward. He did not mind the cold so much so long as he could walk through it.

It was an eight-block walk from the station to McGill's.

After six blocks, he fell in step about fifty yards behind another man. The man heading the same direction. He sensed the other man's walking pace and rhythm. Jack Regan was a quick, strong walker and he estimated he would overtake the man in another three blocks, if there were another three blocks left. But there weren't because the bar was on the next block.

He saw the man in front of him slow and turn into the bar.

Okay. Well, he'd be serving him drinks then.

Regan kept walking.

And, a few seconds later, saw the man come back out.

Hmmm.

The man was backing away, looking into the bar and shaking his head. Then he turned and started to walk back toward Regan.

Regan stopped him.

"Hey," Regan said, his voice gentle. He was a big man and he did not want to frighten the fellah. "Why didn't you go in?"

"It's closed."

Regan looked up at the street. There it

was, McGill's, the sign on and everything. It was only nine thirty.

Regan said, "The sign says it's open."

"That's what I told the guy. He said it was closed."

Regan said, "What guy?"

"Some guy."

Regan thought of Darrell, their cook. He said, "A young fellah, with jeans and a T-shirt?"

"No, some guy in a leather jacket. He was an asshole."

The man walked off.

Jack Regan stood still, looking at the light emanating from McGill's. He felt his heartbeat quicken and he thought of Kate in there, but he made himself back away and put his back to the building. Then he moved back, away from the bar.

He rounded the block and came back up the alleyway, sticking to the sides. He got to the rear fire door. He looked at the door for a moment, then stepped back about ten yards. From his coat pocket he removed a Colt 1911 .45 and racked the slide and put a round in the chamber. He moved back to the fire door. He took his keys out and slowly unlocked it.

At the back of McGill's there was an area that had a storeroom and a small office.

Between that area and the bar was another door. Usually, that second door was closed because they didn't want customers looking in there. If there were men in the bar now who meant to do him harm and that door was open, they would see him, maybe even hear him open the fire door. But there was nothing else he could do.

Slowly, Regan cracked the fire door open. He let it hang there for a moment. Then he widened the crack until it became a space he could step through. Then he stepped through that space and pulled the door behind him.

It was dark. Good. The second door was closed. Regan stood still and let his eyes adjust to the darkness. He could hear music from the jukebox now. Faint. Sinatra singing . . . what? "I Didn't Know What Time It Was." Singing, "Warm, like the month of May it was . . ." They only had two Sinatra songs on the jukebox. Most of the customers these days had no idea about Sinatra. Kids. The other song was "Somethin' Stupid." It had been on the jukebox when he and Kate returned from their wedding. Kate behind the bar in her bridal gown . . .

Regan stepped quietly to the second door and looked through the small dirty window. He saw a man sitting at the bar, near the front door. Black leather jacket. The man's back was to him. Then he saw Kate in the middle of the bar, closer to him. Her hands on the bar. She was standing still. Something made him hesitate, made him reluctant to charge out the door and shoot the leather jacketed man in the back.

Quietly, he opened the door and stepped into the bar. Then he stood in front of the door. He took two steps forward. Then another. Kate was on his right, about thirty feet ahead of him.

She turned slightly, catching him. Then turned her head a little more. Her expression did not change and her shoulders did not move. She looked at him for no more than two seconds. Then she turned back and stared straight ahead of her.

The booth, Regan thought. There's a second one in the booth. It had to be what she was telling him. She wasn't going to be able to give him anything else.

Regan moved his right foot and then his left. Tense, his stomach tight, he took some comfort in the music that hopefully muffled his presence and told him that it was a grand thing to be alive and hers alone, and he moved closer, as if in rhythm, keeping his steps quiet, the .45 in his right hand, loose, but fingers ready to close and squeeze . . .

And now Kate was turning away from him, looking at the leather jacketed man at the front, subconsciously making the person in the booth look that way as well because now she was ready for it too . . . and now Regan was eight feet from the booth, two more steps — one —

Regan swung in front of the booth, watched the eyes of the man wearing a porkpie hat go wide as Regan pointed the .45 and shot him twice in the chest. The porkpie man hammered back into the corner, dead, and Regan turned as Kate ducked behind the bar and Regan walked quickly toward the leather jacketed man, who was turning now. Regan shot him in the shoulder and Regan saw the man's gun flip up into the air and hit the ground before he did. The man reaching for it on the ground and Regan put another round in the man's back, heard it go through and boom into the floor.

Then Regan was standing over him.

The man in the leather jacket was still breathing.

"Kate," Regan said. "Kate! The one in the booth. Is he dead?"

"Yeah."

"Get his shotgun."

Regan kicked the man on the ground.

"Turn over boy, so I can get a look at you." Regan kicked him again. "Come on."

"I can't."

Regan crouched down and put the muzzle of the gun against the man's rib cage. He turned him over.

Sean said, "Christ." He was spitting out words. "Where did you come from?" He spoke as a gracious loser does at a card game. He seemed almost to be smiling.

Sean Rizza.

Regan said, "I guess Max made some calls, huh?"

"That he did, Jack." Sean Rizza shuddered. A moment later, he was able to speak again. "I'm sorry. It's my brother, Jack. It's blood."

"Yeah," Regan said. "It's blood."

Sean gasped for a few seconds. After he got air, he said, "Jack, I'm sorry about her. About your — wife . . . We weren't going to hurt her . . . I swear."

"Ah, Sean. I wish I could believe that." Regan turned to see Kate putting the shotgun on the bar. Her hands were shaking, but she wasn't showing much stress beyond that. She was a tough one.

Regan turned back to Sean and said, "You ready?"

Sean took a few more gasping breaths.

"Yeah," he said. "Go ahead."

The people in the storage room winced as they heard one more gunshot.

NINETEEN

The call went out as shots fired, and they dispatched at least four units to the bar down the street from the man who dialed 911. Three or four distinct pops, maybe more. Then nothing.

Two units converged and then a third in front of McGill's. The patrol officers got out and the senior officer told them to hold back for a moment. They drew their service weapons, sidearms mostly, one of them holding a riot gun. They waited until the senior officer mentally crossed himself and led them in.

Moments later, there was the sound of frightened men swearing but not quite shouting at the sight of the first dead man on the floor, face up in a pool of blood, shot in the head for starters. Seconds later they found the other dead man, a fat guy with two gunshots to the chest, one of which had gone through his heart.

They didn't see anyone else.

They called out for others and felt some relief when they heard voices calling out from a storeroom in the back. More than one of the officers dreaded finding a pile of shot up corpses in there, but didn't and were thankful. But the adrenaline was still running and hands holding weapons shook until they searched the entire place and found only a woman in the kitchen tied up in a chair with a bar towel tied around her mouth so she couldn't cry out. They took the towel out of her mouth and she told them she was the manager and co-owner and she thanked Jesus, Mary, and Joseph that they had come.

Outside, another patrol cruiser raced by, lights flashing. Then it was gone.

Regan stepped out from behind a dumpster, checked the street to see that it was clear, saw that it was, and ran across to another alley.

He went down a series of these, not quite running, not quite walking, but moving quickly until he got to the train station. Boarded the next El that came without looking which one it was. He stayed on the train for the next two stops, then got off at the third.

There was more traffic and bustle at that stop and Regan felt better, slipping in among people and the city. He walked to the Jewel grocery store and looked for an older model car that wouldn't have a burglar alarm. He found one, a 1977 Oldsmobile, red with a peeling vinyl top. It was easy to steal.

Five minutes later, he was on the Eisenhower Expressway, heading west on business.

TWENTY

They sat at a table in the upstairs room of a bar where they could have more privacy. Jimmy Rizza thought it would be better to meet and talk in Mike's house or even his apartment, but Mike Dillon liked to move around. He had been that way ever since Jimmy had known him. Dillon liked to be out in the open, facing the front doors of places, like Wild Bill Hickok used to, until he didn't and he died. Dillon moved because he had enough of walls, whether or not the walls had ears.

He had spent nine years in prison, starting when he was in his mid-twenties. When he first got there he often started fights and, as a result, spent long stretches in solitary confinement. Years of being alone in a small cell with double steel doors and no window for twenty-three hours a day. No work, no education, meals alone, and maybe one hour in a dog run outside. Nine years training himself to stay sane, nine years surviving. He survived by thinking about the future and staying angry at the people who had put him there, feeding on that anger, but keeping it in. Learning to do the time and not letting the time do him. Disciplining himself to think about things beyond the prison walls.

Dillon believed that he had not spent that time in vain. Before he went in, he had made too many mistakes. He had not thought things out. Acted on impulse, started fights at the wrong time with the wrong people. Started fights with cops, never working with them. And then he had nine years with nothing to do but think. When he was allowed out of solitary confinement, he started to read books for the first time. He read biographies of Julius Caesar and Machiavelli, before moving onto American history. He read Grant's autobiography and it opened up an interest in the Civil War. He liked to read about generals of the North and South. They were brave men, but they weren't chumps either, eager to self-destruct. They were fierce fighters, but they knew when not to strike too. They knew the value of diplomacy. Dillon studied and he thought and he came out a different man, yet in many ways the same. A controlled sociopath. He swore he would never go back to prison.

When he was released he returned to Chicago and became an enforcer for John Zanatelli. He killed the people Zans wanted killed, but always with the goal of branching out on his own. He succeeded in this within a couple of years and soon had his own operation, quietly competing with Zans, yet not acknowledging it.

Now, sitting at the upstairs room in the St. Louis saloon, Dillon remembered the times in Chicago when they always had music turned up loud whenever they talked business for fear they were being recorded. Bugs everywhere. Bugs in the walls, in the ceilings, in his home and his car. The guy had told him to watch out for it and he had.

It started to wear on you, living like that. It got to where you didn't want to talk to anyone unless music was turned up or someone was driving a jackhammer nearby. It beat being in prison, but it still worked on you.

Two hours earlier, Jimmy had made the call. Two hours and twenty minutes before that, Max had called Jimmy. Between the two calls, Jimmy had called Dillon and given him the news.

Now they were waiting for confirmation from Chicago that it was done. Jimmy Rizza was letting the waiting time work on him.

Jimmy said, "You sure we didn't over-react?"

Dillon said, "Why do you think that?"

Jimmy said, "Jack's a good guy."

"Sure," Dillon said. "Jack's all right. But he doesn't work freelance, you know that."

"Yeah, but . . ."

"Yeah, but what? He asked Max where you were. Jack wouldn't do that unless he had a reason."

"I never done nothing to Jack."

"That's the point," Dillon said. "He's been retained, see."

Jimmy Rizza gripped his beer bottle, released the grip, and twisted the bottle around slowly. He did this for a couple of revolutions. Then he said, "You think he's working for Zans?"

Dillon had no doubt Jack was working for Zans. It was the only thing he was certain of because it was the only thing that made sense. Zans had reason and he had the money to hire Jack Regan to get it done.

But how had Zans found out that he had fingered him? The only ones who knew were him and Jimmy and a handful of feds begging for information.

Dillon decided it wasn't Jimmy's business what he thought. In answer to Jimmy's question, he merely shrugged.

After a moment, Jimmy said, "Well, what difference does it make? Sean will take care of it."

Dillon said, "Don't worry about things you can't control."

Jimmy Rizza went back to twisting his bottle.

TWENTY-ONE

Regan parked the car a few blocks from the house in Lake Forest. He walked through a series of yards, walked in darkness. When he got to the house, he unlocked the door to the garage with the same steel ruler he had used on the car. He was worried about the car now because the car was old and shabby and even though it was parked several blocks away it would stand out in an affluent neighborhood like this. A homeowner might see it and call the police to have it towed away. He might have to leave the car and find another way home, but he would think about that later.

There were two Mercedeses in the garage, a white roadster, and the SUV. Max was here, as Regan had thought he would be. It was good because Regan didn't have much time. The McGill's killings were about forty minutes old now and they would probably lead the ten o'clock news. A few minutes from now. If Max saw it on television, he would panic. Call Jimmy again or maybe even get desperate enough to call the police, though it was hard to imagine what he could tell the police. *Dude, I tried to have this guy clipped and it just totally blew up in my fucking face.*

It was a big house, older with red brick. Once inside, Regan could tell they had spent the money fixing it up. Could easily spend three hundred grand fixing one of these old mansions up. Money that could be used to buy another newer house entirely, with better plumbing and more efficient heating systems.

There were toys in the living room. The man had children. Shit, Regan thought. Where were they? He moved through the house, into the study and another living room. He searched all the rooms downstairs and didn't find anyone. Then he went upstairs and checked all the rooms there. No one. Regan went to the master bedroom. The television was on. Regan looked at a door that he thought led to a bathroom. The door was closed and light emanated from under it. Regan stood to the right of the door.

He heard the toilet flush and Max came out. Regan hit him on the ear with the .45.

Max stumbled and fell on the floor.

Max looked up at Regan.

For a moment neither one of them said anything.

Then Regan said, "Where's your family?"

"I sent them away."

"You called Jimmy, didn't you?"

"I don't know what you're —"

"Max, they're dead. Sean and the guy he brought with him. They're both dead."

Max squeezed his eyes shut. When he opened them Jack Regan was still pointing that .45 at him. He said, "How?"

"I got lucky," Regan said. He didn't like to lie.

"It was Sean's idea."

Regan didn't like liars either.

"Max, they were going to kill me and Kate. We both know that. You brought my wife into it. Now, being a sporting man, I'm going to give you a chance to save *your* wife's life. If it means anything to you, and it better 'cause she's the mother of your children." Regan said, "Who did you call?"

"I called Sean."

Regan shook his head.

"No. Sean wouldn't do it for you. He'd only do it for Jimmy. He told me that."

"What else did he tell you?"

"That's between us," Regan said. "You

called Jimmy, didn't you?"

After a moment, Max said, "I had to."

"No you didn't, Max. You could have given me what I needed and left it alone. You made the wrong play. But you can protect your family now. All you have to do is write down the number you called."

"Okay," Max said. "Let me get a pen and paper."

Regan saw Max look toward the dresser drawer.

"Stay there," Regan said. He walked over to the dresser and opened the drawer Max had glanced at. Too easy. In the drawer, beneath the clothes, was a .38 revolver.

"Max," he said, sighing disappointment. Regan put the .38 in his coat pocket. He found a pen on a table and a paperback book. Nora Roberts. He tossed the book and the pen to Max. "Write it on that," Regan said.

Max wrote the telephone digits on the inside cover of the book.

"Let me see it," Regan said and Max slid it over to him. A telephone number with a 314 prefix. St. Louis.

Max said, "Listen, I think we can work some —"

Regan took the .38 out of his pocket and shot Max twice in the chest. Watched him as he slumped over. Regan moved closer and put another round in his head.

When he got back to town, he threw both the .45 and the .38 into the Chicago River.

TWENTY-TWO

The door was latched when Hastings got home, and he had to identify himself before Amy took it off the hinge and let him in. She was watching television with her friend Jennifer. There was a commercial on they'd all seen before. A guy and his girlfriend frolicking in Rome, the guy pointing out the girl's mom and dad sitting on a step nearby — what are they doing here? — then pulling out an engagement ring and proposing to her as she's overcome with emotion and the parents and about fifty total strangers stand up and applaud. Hastings wondered what woman on planet earth would forgive a guy for pulling a stunt like that. Then it was back to the local newscast, a handsome young man saying, let's go to high school soccer. Amy's friend turned to watch. The girl liked boys who played sports. It was not difficult to see that Jennifer's home life was kind of crappy and that was why she spent so much time over at their house. Hastings thought she was a nice kid. He remembered the time Amy had told Jennifer that he used to be a baseball player and the girl seemed to have trouble buying it. He resisted the urge to tell her he had once been cool.

In the dining room, Hastings took off his jacket and began emptying his pockets. Putting cell phone and checkbook and keys on the table. Then he found the two hundred dollars in twenties.

Shit.

He remembered offering it to the woman. And then somehow the subject got changed and she hadn't taken it. He tried to remember if she had refused to take it. If she had refused to take it, he could put it back in his pocket and forget about it. Do that and give it no more thought. He tried to remember.

No . . . she had never openly refused to take it.

So, now what?

If she had meant to accept it, but just didn't say so and he kept it, it would be a form of stealing. Worse, she would think that he was stiffing her because she had given him heat about the way he handled Kody. She had all but said he was corrupt.

Hadn't she?

Or had she only implied that he was trying to cover up for another crooked cop? And it had made him mad. So if he called her now and offered her the money, she'd probably accuse him of trying to bribe her. So . . . the wisest thing was just to keep the money and forget about it.

Hastings said, "Fuck."

From the next room, Amy scolded him. "Da-*ad.*"

"Sorry, honey."

Hastings walked to the kitchen and called Sam Hall and asked for the woman's number.

Sam said, "It's almost ten thirty, George. Couldn't you have called tomorrow?"

"Sorry."

"You're not going to ask her out, are you? I doubt she'd date a cop."

"I'm not — just give me the number, Sam."

Carol McGuire answered on the fourth ring. She did not sound like she had been sleeping.

"Hello?"

"Hi. This is George Hastings. The detective."

"Oh, hi." She said, "What's the matter?"

"Well, nothing really. It's just that I never

184

paid you." He said, "The two hundred, I mean."

"*You* were going to pay me?"

"Yeah, don't you remember? I brought it up when we first met."

"You were going to pay me."

Hastings got a beer out of the refrigerator, opened it.

"Yes," he said.

The McGuire woman didn't say anything at first.

Then, "Don't worry about it."

"Well . . . no, we had an agreement. You came down to jail and O.R.'d him out. I don't want you to get stiffed."

"Really, don't worry about it."

Hastings shifted on his feet. "Listen," he said, "I don't feel comfortable keeping the money. I'd feel better if you just took it."

"Why?"

It put him back on his heels for a moment because he wasn't ready for it. Why, she asked, and there was something in the way she said it. A lawyer's question, perhaps, but she had not used a lawyer's voice when she asked it, which makes a difference. And then he was conscious of himself, standing alone in the kitchen.

"I don't know," Hastings said. "Pride, I guess."

"Yours?"

"Yes."

"You don't want me to think badly of you."

"No."

"You don't want me to think you're a crook or a squirrel."

"No, I don't."

"You want my respect. Is that it?"

"Maybe that's it."

There was a silence between them as Hastings stood still.

The woman said, "Why would you care what I think?"

"I don't know," Hastings said.

"Don't you?"

Christ, Hastings thought. What is this? Woman pushing him into a corner.

"I hadn't really thought — look, I'm not a —"

"Why did you call me?"

"I told you why I called you."

"You could've just mailed me a check."

"I may do that," Hastings said, some irritation in his voice.

Carol McGuire said, "If it's what you want to do."

"Or," Hastings said, "we could have dinner or . . . something."

"Dinner."

"If you want," Hastings said. He wasn't sure how this had happened. He waited for the woman to end this discomfort and tell him she didn't date cops and to stick the two hundred dollars up his ass.

"I don't know," she said. "Why don't we just have a drink, see how that goes?"

TWENTY-THREE

Driving to work the next morning, Hastings got another call on his cell phone. A number he didn't recognize, but he answered anyway.

"Hello?"

"George, it's me."

"Hey," Hastings said. "You calling me from the hospital bed?"

"Yeah," Klosterman said. "A man can only watch so much *Regis and Kelly*."

"Who are they?"

"Oh don't give me that 'I'm unaware of pop culture' shit. You know who they are." Klosterman said, "You ever watch this show called *The View*?"

"No," Hastings said. Telling the truth now.

"It's this show with Barbara Walters and these four women. Usually just the four women. Three older ladies and this young hot-looking one the others all seem to hate. Sometimes I watch it with the mute on and

188

just study the body language. It tells you a lot."

"You must be bored."

"Yeah, I'm going fucking crazy." Klosterman said, "That case with the cop murders, is it yours?"

"Yeah," Hastings said. "I meant to tell you." Feeling bad now.

"That's all right," Klosterman said. "Tell me about it."

"Well, it's pretty fucking awful. Two cops machine-gunned. Forty-eight hours have passed by and I don't really have solid leads."

"How about manpower?"

"I got Murph, Rhodes, Cain. We're all working on it."

"Hmmm."

Hastings knew Joe wanted out now, wanted to be working the case. Hastings knew the feeling of needing a mission in life.

Klosterman said, "How's Cain working out?"

"Oh . . . not too bad, actually."

"Yeah?"

"He's an asshole. We drove to Marion together to interview a suspect . . . long fucking drive."

"Yeah?"

"The guy's a talker." Hastings said, "But he's not stupid. He's got pretty good instincts actually. He could be a very good detective if he'd mellow out a bit, not take himself so seriously."

"So . . . you're in love with him?"

"You've been watching too much TV." Hastings said, "You know this guy in narcotics, Justin Elliott?"

"Black guy?"

"Yeah."

"Yeah, I know him."

"What about him?"

"Ah, a bit of a peacock. My understanding is he's all right."

"Had kind of a run-in with him. Turns out, he and Deputy Hummel used to work together."

"County?"

"No. Hummel worked undercover, deep. Played a big part in convicting Steve Treats. Treats is the guy Cain and I interviewed yesterday."

"What was Treats in for?"

"Meth dealer. Hummel got to know him undercover, came out of the wilderness, and testified against him. Elliott thinks Treats had Hummel killed."

"Yeah? What do you think?"

"I don't know. When we went to interview

Treats —"

"Treats agreed to see you?"

"Yeah."

"Without a lawyer?"

"Yeah," Hastings said, "let me finish. Treats saw us and told us that Hummel was dirty. Taking payoffs, selling cases."

"Ah."

"I checked it out though. Remember Kody?"

"Oh, yeah."

"Kody says Hummel never took anything."

Klosterman said, "I think Kody would know."

"Yeah, that's what I think. God, I hope he's right, though."

"Who, Kody?"

"Yeah."

"Yeah, I know what you mean," Klosterman said. "I'd hate to read about another dirty cop. But, like I said, if this Hummel were dirty, Kody would've probably known. Why don't you send Murph and Rhodes out, roust up some of our informants on the street. See what they've heard."

"Yeah, I'm going to do that."

"What about the car the guy was driving?"

"What — the one the deputies pulled over?"

"Yeah. Did it give you anything?"

"No. No prints. It was stolen."

"Didn't the deputies know that?"

"No. They didn't call in the tag."

"Oh, Jesus."

"Yeah, I know. But I'm not going to second-guess the guys."

"Because they're dead?"

"Look, man. We've all made fuckups. You remember patrol."

"Yeah, but . . ."

"Look, Joe." Hastings paused, made sure his tone was respectful. "Don't do this cop thing, okay? We could have made the same mistake and then we'd've been killed. No one's immune."

"From death?"

"From fucking up."

"All right, all right." Klosterman backed off. Then he said, "Listen, let me help, will you? I'm really going nuts here."

Hastings almost said, what can you do? But remembered himself and didn't. He wanted to tell the man that he had already helped by being the great sounding board he was. That he needed this. But it would sound patronizing, even though it wasn't.

Hastings said, "You got pen and paper?"

"I can get some."

"The car was stolen from the parking lot

of Schnucks off Laclede Station Road. Can you make some calls, see if there's maybe some security videotapes?"

"Be glad to."

"Thanks."

Hastings was parking the car now.

He said, "Hey, you still there?"

"Yeah."

"Do you know a woman named Carol McGuire?"

"From the P.D.'s office?"

"She used to be."

"Yeah, I know her. She cross-examined me once on a robbery case."

"Really?" Hastings wondered if it would be proper to ask what she was like.

But Klosterman spoke anyway. "She was pretty fucking mean. Why are you asking about her?"

"Well . . . it's a long story. I'm having a drink with her tonight."

"You're what?"

"Well . . ."

"Jesus," Klosterman said. "This is what happens when I leave you alone."

"Go back to Regis and Kelly Lee," Hastings said.

TWENTY-FOUR

A fashionable restaurant in the Central West End. White tablecloths and short histories of French wine written on the wall behind the bar.

Frank Cahalin stood and offered his hand as the man approached the table.

Cain said, "Frank Cahalin?"

"Yes," Frank said. The men shook hands and Frank offered the man a seat. Frank said, "You go by Bob, Robert, what?"

"Bobby's fine."

"Great." They situated themselves at the table. Frank said, "You been here before?"

"Yes," Cain said. "I'm from St. Louis."

"Is that right?"

"Yes, sir. You?"

"No. I'm from Chicago."

"And they posted you down here?"

"Well," Frank said, "they offered me the SAC position here, not in Chicago. But I was in Chicago most of my service."

Bobby Cain said, "SAC means —"

"Special Agent in Charge."

"Oh. Well."

Frank made a throwaway gesture of modesty. Special Agent in Charge at his age. It was impressive and they both knew it.

Cain was surprised when Cahalin had called him. The FBI bigwig saying people had said Cain was one of the most promising detectives in the Department. Mr. Cahalin had said that he was considering putting together a joint task force of municipal law enforcement and federal agents and he needed to interview around. Cain had heard the words "joint task force" before, though he'd never actually been a part of one. He told Mr. Cahalin that that sounded interesting, and what was the joint task force for? Mr. Cahalin said that they could discuss that at lunch, but the important thing was that they get together.

Now they were at a nice place, and the joint task force didn't seem to be anywhere in sight. Frank said, "Tell me about yourself."

Bobby Cain did so. Where he went to school, when he became a cop, what drew him into law enforcement. A little bit about his wife and kids. The cautious thought-out things people say when they're being interviewed for a job. Lunch at a nice restaurant, but the FBI Special Agent in Charge had called him and said they should meet and talk.

Frank said, "You go to law school?"

"No," Cain said. "But I plan to."

Frank shook his head. "You don't have to go to law school to work for the Bureau. It helps, but it's not a requirement."

"Well —"

"It's good if you want to. But it's not necessary."

"Okay," Cain said. He sipped his water and went back into character. He said, "I understand if you work for the fe— , the Bureau, they won't let you stay in your hometown."

"Ah," Frank said, "there's ways around that. Would you want to stay here?"

"Well, yeah. Sort of. I mean, I've got family here. I mean, eventually."

"I know what you mean," Frank said. "I'm a Chicagoan myself. Huge White Sox fan, love the lake. You know how it is. The Bureau hired me out of law school. And you know where they sent me?"

"Where?"

"Mississippi."

"Yeah?"

"Oh, man. I thought I would die. The

heat, the boredom. Try getting deep pan pizza in Jackson, Mississippi. Right?" Frank smiled an obliging chuckle out of Bobby. One of the costs of ambition. "But," Frank said, "it was only for about two years. Then I got posted back to Chicago. Best day of my life."

"Yeah?"

"I mean, it was home for me. But it was also where the action was. The work itself was fulfilling. You know what I mean?"

"Oh, yeah," Cain said. "That's what it's all about. The fulfillment."

"The thing is, if you choose a career in the Bureau, ostensibly, you have to go where they send you. But if you've got talent and smarts, eventually you can go where you want. If it's Washington or New York, okay. If it's back here, that's fine too."

Cain nodded his head, as if in thought. When he thought enough time had passed by, he said, "Okay."

The waitress took their orders then left them alone.

Frank said, "So you're a detective."

"Yes, sir."

"Hey. It's Frank."

"Okay." Bobby smiled. "Yeah, I work in homicide."

"Is that right?"

"Yeah."

Frank looked down at his salad, aiming his fork at a tomato. "How do you like that?" he said.

"It's pretty cool."

"And you're a sergeant?"

"Yes."

Frank Cahalin nodded his head, as if impressed but letting Cain know that they were only looking for the top candidates. "Homicide," Frank said, "that's the elite."

"Well, I don't know about that."

"Oh, yeah. If I were in municipal law enforcement, that's where I'd want to be."

Frank did not look at Cain when he said that. It was meant to sting, a little, and he was sure it had. Like, if I couldn't be a doctor, I'd want to be a nurse.

"Yeah, well," Cain said, ". . . it's all right."

Frank said, "Handling anything interesting now?"

"Yeah. You heard about the two county deputies?"

"That's your case?"

"Yeah."

"Man," Frank said. "That was a terrible thing."

"Yeah, I know."

"How's it going? Any leads?"

"Well, a few. Apparently, one of the deputies used to work in narcotics. Undercover. He helped put a major dealer away."

"Really? And you guys see a connection?"

"Well, we don't know."

Frank said, "What don't you know?"

"My lieutenant's skeptical."

"Who's your lieutenant?"

"George Hastings. You heard of him?"

Frank thought for a moment. "Was he the primary on that doctor case last year?"

"Yeah. The doctor that murdered a judge. Well, actually the guy — Sullivan was his name — he paid someone else to kill the judge. Then killed the guy he hired. He — did you read about it?"

"I vaguely recall it."

"The doctor and the judge had been college buddies twenty or so years ago. And back then, the doctor — he wasn't a doctor then, just a college student — he threw some girl off a balcony and killed her. The judge, who was just a kid at the time, he witnessed it. Twenty years later, the judge gets in trouble and he calls the doctor and tells him he wants hush money so he can pay his lawyer. So Sullivan had him killed." Cain said, "It was the lieutenant's case."

Frank Cahalin saw that the young detective was impressed in spite of himself. He didn't like this.

"Is he pretty smart, your lieutenant?"

"Yeah, he knows his — stuff."

"Sure. But we all need help."

"I wasn't involved in it," Cain said. "It was before I was transferred to his division."

"You said your lieutenant was skeptical. About what?"

"The meth dealer that Deputy Hummel testified against. Narcotics thinks he put a contract out on Hummel."

"Who's the dealer?"

"Guy named Steve Treats. White trash crank dealer. He's in Marion now, serving out a long sentence."

"What's Hastings's problem with it?"

"I'm not sure, actually."

"What do *you* think?"

"Me?"

"Yeah, you. What do you think?"

"Well, I mean —"

"Listen," Frank said, "you want a career in law enforcement, you've got to learn to trust your instincts. Seriously."

"Well . . ."

"Do you think this Treats was behind it?"

"I think there's something to it. Maybe."

"Then you have to develop it."

Bobby Cain became uncomfortable. He said, "Listen, he's my lieutenant."

"Let me be crystal clear about something:

I am not counseling insubordination. No, sir. No one understands better than me the importance of chain of command. But in the same aspect, you've got to develop your leads. Police work is not all interrogations and arrests, okay? It's intelligence, information. All this CSI technical bullshit, it's secondary. At the end of the day, you got to trust your gut. Two cops got killed. You owe it to them to give it your best."

Bobby Cain looked at his fork and knife, the knife still clean.

Frank Cahalin sighed. "Look," he said, "pardon me if I'm speaking out of school. It's city's case, not FBI's. I just want to give you the benefit of my experience, that's all. Maybe it's worth listening to, maybe it's not."

"No," Cain said, "it's worth something. It's worth a lot."

Frank was quiet for a few moments. He seemed to study Cain.

Frank said, "I think you've got a great career ahead of you. I look at you and I envy you. Here I am with this big fancy-schmancy title pushing papers around on a desk. I'll retire in a couple of years, head up security at some big corporation, draw a fat salary, and hang out with the rich people. But who am I kidding; that's not me. I can live in the rich neighborhoods with the doctors and the lawyers, but I'm still just an Irish cop at heart. You know? None of it means anything. You, you're doing real police work."

Cain wanted to ask, what are the names of some of these corporations?

Instead he said, "It's just one case."

"I'll be frank with you." Frank smiled at himself. "There's a place for you at the Bureau. You're *real,* you know what I'm saying. Ninety percent of the guys we interview, they're candy-asses, coming out of Catholic law schools. Steel-rim glasses, Joseph Banks suits . . . they're chops. You, you're the real deal."

"Thank you, Frank."

"But I want you to stay where you are until you get this case cleared. You come to us, officially, after doing that and you start out with a real advantage. You start out at the head of the class." Frank said, "Can you do that for me?"

"Okay, Frank."

"These deputy murders," Frank said, "anytime you want to talk about it, you call me?"

"Okay."

"I'm serious, Bobby. I want to help."

"Okay. But, you know, I don't want to

bother you."

"Hey," Frank said, "it's no bother. We're all cops, aren't we?"

The waitress came back. Frank smiled at her as he signed for the check. Cain didn't say anything. She left and Frank said, "We should have dinner sometime. Hang out with a bunch of fat feds. You a wine drinker?"

"Sure," Cain said. He had had some at a wedding months ago.

"I've got a bottle of '66 Montrachet. You got to try it."

TWENTY-FIVE

Hastings parked the Jaguar at the front of the lot of the Ace Hardware store on Manchester. Got out and watched traffic go by. It was around one o'clock in the afternoon, sun threatening to crack through the clouds. He squinted something like disapproval. It had been dark on the night of the murders and he wanted to sense it as the deputies had sensed it, but he was out here now and it was better for him to be able to see things.

This was the place where the deputies had pulled over the young white male driving the Chevy Suburban. They had called in the tag on the Suburban at 2043 hours, found nothing on the guy and let him go. They went 10-8 — back in service — at 2058 hours. Two minutes shy of nine o'clock.

They were working the second shift, four to midnight.

Hastings had worked that shift when he was on patrol. Patrol. A lot of tedium, then all at once, action. Then coming back down to routine, more tedium. Second shift; the peak hours for criminal activity. Yet he had pulled his service weapon only once when he worked that shift. Dispatch had told them that county deputies needed backup on a guy threatening to commit suicide. They got to the guy's house and the guy immediately bolted inside and Hastings and his partner followed the two deputies inside. What happened next happened very quickly. Within the count of five, all of the cops were standing in a bedroom doorway as the caller stood nearby waving a Samurai sword at them then at himself and then back at them. They drew their weapons and shouted orders: *put the sword down, now, put the sword down,* and the guy not only didn't comply with commands, but *leveled* that fucking sword and rushed them, screaming like Howard Dean, and they shot him.

Hastings had been behind two of the officers as they all backed up at once and someone tripped and as the gunfire erupted they all tumbled into the hallway like the Marx Brothers in *A Night at the Opera.* Hastings never discharged his weapon and when it was done he gave thanks and praise that he hadn't accidentally put a round in another officer's back. The swordsman died, of course, which was what he wanted.

Hastings felt ashamed later because he hadn't been in front. But Jerry, his partner — who had been in front of him — told him in a tired voice to shut up because the whole thing had happened so quickly and there was no time to see who should stand where. They were in the house and then they were in the bedroom doorway and then it was happening and that was that.

They were hailed as heroes. Killing a guy who wanted to be killed. But, *goddamn it,* it had been close. Hastings remembered seeing the sword about two feet from his partner after it was done. Two, three more feet to close the distance and drive the sword right through Jerry's midsection. It could have easily happened, but it didn't. No cops died that night.

Hastings looked at his notebook.

10-8 at 2058.

Hastings got back into the Jaguar. Started it, paused at the road to wait for traffic, then pulled out and drove west on Manchester.

Went that way for 1.8 miles, trying to feel a time when a Nissan Pathfinder came into his view. Slowed at the street where it happened and turned right and stopped.

He pulled over to the curb, pictured the Pathfinder's brake lights reddening as it pulled over and stopped.

They had not called in the tag.

Hastings got out of the car and stood by his door.

Just then his cell phone rang.

"Hastings."

"It's Joe."

"Hey, what's up?"

"I called the store security. No videotape of the parking lot."

"Shit. Well, thanks for trying." Hastings said, "I'm at the crime scene now."

"Yeah? What do you think?"

"I think they pulled over a guy in the Pathfinder, and then another vehicle came along and someone in that vehicle shot them."

"How many guys in the second car?"

"I think two."

"I think two too."

Hastings said, "Why do you think that?"

"If it's one, it would have taken too much time, given the deputies time to react. I don't think these were thrill seekers. I think they were professional, experienced killers and they had a plan."

Hastings read from his notepad. "The Pathfinder was reported stolen from the

Schnucks at 1722 hours. So . . ."

"So it would seem it was stolen for this purpose. No joyriders."

Hastings stood in the road. It led north into a neighborhood, quiet street with trees on the sides, most of the leaves gone now. He looked behind himself at Manchester Road. He said, "I think they came off Manchester, shot the guys, picked up the driver of the Pathfinder, and continued north."

Klosterman said, "That would make sense."

"Three guys," Hastings said. With guns and a thought-out plan. Worse odds than a lunatic with a sword. He said, "The guys in the second car would have been waiting somewhere. Probably followed the deputies for a while."

"Predators," Klosterman said.

Hastings began walking north.

"If it wasn't kicks, they must have had a reason."

Klosterman said, "Political statement?" He didn't sound convinced himself.

"Here?" Hastings said.

"Just thinking out loud."

Neither Hastings nor Klosterman was the product of an especially politically active generation. They had once passed by a bunch of college students gathered on the beautiful grounds of Washington University on their way to interview a witness. The kids, with arms linked, were singing "We Shall Overcome" for some reason, and Klosterman said, "Overcome what? Capital gains tax?"

If not politics, then what? What would motivate someone to murder two policemen? Hastings had worked homicide for many years. He had handled cases where people got killed because they wouldn't give up the television remote control. Had seen toddlers murdered by their own mothers because they wouldn't stop crying. Had seen things that kept him awake at night alternating between wondering if there was a God who could allow such cruelty and hoping He did exist and that victims now rested in a better place.

Yet in his entire career he had not seen policemen murdered merely because they were policemen. It was either luck or some quirk of American society.

"George?"

"Huh?"

"You still there?"

"Yeah, sorry."

"So . . . what are you thinking?"

Klosterman, sounding like a woman now,

in bed afterward. Like most men, he'd be thinking who was on *Letterman.* Hastings shook his head. It had been a while since he'd been with a woman.

Hastings said, "I don't have any ideas. Two cops killed under circumstances that look thought out, planned. And I don't know why." He said, "I'd like to think Steve Treats was behind it. But that's just a theory. There's no evidence to support that he did it."

"There's motive," Klosterman said.

"Steve Treats is a little punk. He made some money, rode high for a while. But he's no kingpin."

"You think Elliott wants you to hang it on Treats anyway?"

"You mean, even if he's innocent?"

"Yeah."

Most cops, including Hastings, developed a mind-set about criminals. Basically, that if they weren't guilty of the criminal charge filed, they were surely guilty of another one not filed. It was hard not to think that way. But if you weren't careful it could lead to fabricated cases and embarrassing cross-examinations in court.

Hastings said, "I wouldn't put it past him. But if we succeed in hanging it on Treats, the real killers will get away."

"And if they do," Klosterman said, "you know what they're going to think, don't you?"

"What?"

"That they're smarter than you."

Hastings pictured his partner smiling, jabbing at his ego.

"That's right," he said. "And you know how I feel about that."

"Call me if you need me," Klosterman said.

TWENTY-SIX

Hastings got to the bar at the Cheshire Inn fifteen minutes early. He took a seat at the bar and ordered a cup of coffee. He was still flipping through his notebook when Carol got there.

She was dressed in lawyer clothes this time. Sort of: a gray tweed skirt and a white sweater with a jacket on top. She said hello and asked if they could sit at a table. They took one near the fireplace. She took off her jacket and set it on a chair, and Hastings found himself looking at her again.

She looked at the coffee cup sitting on the saucer.

"You don't drink?" she said.

"No, I drink." He set the saucer on the table. "I mean, not much."

She ordered a glass of wine and he ordered a Jack Daniel's on ice. Hastings felt a little awkward, the coffee cup and the whiskey glass somehow reflecting indecision on his part. He could throw the coffee cup in the fireplace like he was Douglas Fairbanks. Then she would think he was crazy and leave.

Hastings said, "Did you and Kody talk again?"

"Yes."

"Did it go okay?"

"Yeah. He should be able to get a decent plea."

"Good."

They were both quiet for a moment, conscious of how they had met through Kody and the accusations they had made after.

Hastings said, "I guess we never met before. I mean, we never saw each other in court or anything like that."

"No."

Hastings said, "My partner knows you."

"Who's that?"

"Joe Klosterman. He's a sergeant in homicide."

"I thought you were a lieutenant?"

"I am. He's still my partner." Hastings said, "He's in the hospital now."

"What's wrong?"

"He had a tumor removed. They think he's going to be all right."

Carol said, "He's a sergeant detective?"

"Yes."

"Got a mustache?"

"Yeah."

"I think I remember him." She smiled. "He say something mean about me?"

"Look, I wasn't — I just asked him if he knew you, that's all."

"I know."

"But, yeah, he said that you were a pretty good lawyer."

Carol said, "That's mean?"

"It is from our perspective."

The woman said, "My ex-husband, who's a lawyer, he once represented a police officer in a divorce. I won't tell you who. And the officer was pretty happy with what Edward had done for him and when it was done, he took Edward to . . . what's that cop bar?"

"Dunnigan's."

"Yeah, Dunnigan's. And they walk in together, and the police officer says, 'This is my lawyer.' And all the cops, you know, groaned at him. And the cop says, 'Hey, I hate lawyers. All except this one.' Then they all bought him drinks. Edward said he'd never been so flattered."

Or so drunk, Hastings thought. Typically, they served whiskey in jelly jars at Dunnigan's, filled to the top. Cops drank like hill people, with similar consequences thereafter.

"That's nice," Hastings said. "So, you're divorced?"

"Yes. Two years ago." She said, "You?"

"Yeah. Last year."

"I'm sorry," she said. "You have kids?"

"One. A daughter. We have joint custody." Hastings said, "She's a great kid."

"How old?"

"Twelve." Hastings said, "Do you have children?"

"No."

Hastings thought, you could ask her: what happened? How did the marriage end? She might tell him and then expect him to reciprocate and he would have to talk about Eileen and he didn't want to do that. They'd be starting with the most intimate and, frankly, painful subjects and then perhaps be stuck with the prospect of having opened up to a total stranger you may not even like that much. Better to talk about movies or baseball, but then those things didn't really interest him much. He was attracted to Carol McGuire but he was pushing forty now, recently divorced, and he didn't know what people did on dates at this point. In a warped way, he wished she had committed or witnessed some crime so he could relax

215

and get down to interrogating her.

Carol said, "It gets better."

"What?"

"Being alone," she said. "It gets better after a while."

"Oh. Yeah, I suppose it does."

After a moment, she said, "Listen, about the other night . . . I'm sorry if I offended you."

"You didn't."

"No, I think I did. I don't . . . like policemen all that much, I'll admit that. But I don't think I was being fair to you. It's just that, you're all so tribal and I've seen — I've been involved in cases where I know cops have lied. That's all."

"Are your clients known for being excessively truthful?"

"No, they're not." She said, "But . . . they haven't taken oaths, have they?"

Hastings frowned.

Carol said, "I won't say anything more like that, okay? I don't — like to fight off duty." She said, "Really, I don't."

Hastings thought he understood. Eventually he said, "No, I don't either."

"I just wanted to let you know where I was coming from. The other night."

"You have."

They looked at each other and then they

looked away from each other. A man and a woman drawn to each other in spite of everything, or maybe because of everything.

Carol said, "I'm sorry about what happened. To those police officers, I mean."

"Thank you."

"Did they have families?"

"One of them did. Wife and children. The other one didn't. He was young, had only been a deputy for a few months. A kid, really."

"He was twenty-four," Carol McGuire said.

"How did you know that?"

"It was in the newspaper."

Hastings wondered why she had said that. Was she telling him he wasn't really a kid? Okay, he was twenty-four, older than most soldiers. Approaching middle age for a professional football player. But, man, to end life at twenty-four.

Hastings said, "I guess it doesn't make any difference."

Carol said, "I didn't mean it like that."

"I know you didn't," he said. Although he hadn't been sure. But her tone was different now. And she was looking at him with an open, frank expression.

Carol said, "May I ask you something?"

"Sure."

"It's somewhat personal."

"That's okay."

She said, "Outside of people working in law enforcement, who do you talk to?"

"My," Hastings said, "that is personal."

"We're alone now."

The place was filling up now. Grad students from Washington University, yuppies from Clayton. Voices and glasses clinking.

Hastings said, "Oh, I don't know. I talk to my daughter. We talk quite a bit, actually."

"Any grown-ups?"

"She's more grown-up than I care to admit."

Carol McGuire frowned. "Come on."

"I guess — well, no one. My wife and I used to talk. She was very supportive."

"I'm not going to ask you what happened."

"It's all right if you do." Hastings said, "She left me."

"Hmmm," Carol said. "Do you mind if I smoke?"

"No, I don't mind."

She took cigarettes and a lighter out of her purse. She lit a cigarette, turned her head sideways to exhale. Her legs folded now.

"Listen," she said. "I was probably a little too cautious earlier."

"What do you mean?"

"When you called and asked me to dinner, I said let's just have a drink. That's what I mean."

"That's understandable. It goes badly and you're still waiting for salads. I guess it can make for a long night. And they never look as good as their pictures on the Internet."

"What?"

"I'm kidding; I've never done that."

The woman smiled. "You had me, there."

Hastings gestured that he had his moments.

"Actually, that's how I met my ex-husband."

"Really?"

Carol McGuire shook her head.

"Okay," Hastings said, "enough of this cute shit. Do you want to have dinner with me or not?"

"Sure," Carol said, "let's get it over with."

Later, plates with half-eaten food had been taken away and fourth drinks were brought back to the table.

Carol McGuire, with a fresh cigarette in hand, leaned forward and placed her lighter in Hastings's hand. He lit her cigarette and set the lighter on the table.

She leaned back and said, "You're full of shit."

"I'm telling you," Hasting said, "I can do it. Any good detective can do that."

"You can look at two people, total strangers, and tell if they're on their first date, and if they've been to bed together? No. You just *think* you can do that."

"It's not like I'm Kreskin. *You* could do that, if you wanted. You see those people over there? . . . No, don't point at them, for Christ's sake. You see her, right. She's pretty and he's handsome. He's also gay. Although he's not ready to acknowledge it. In fact, he probably never will be. He's got money though. I'll bet he's a doctor. And she wants to get married. He wants to get married too. They probably both have children from their first marriages."

"A gay man with children wants to marry a woman? Come on, this isn't 1955."

"My dear, you could pass the most open-minded gay rights legislation in western civilization and guys like that still ain't gonna come out. It's not gonna happen."

"Because people like you don't understand."

Hastings smiled. "Oh, please. You don't know what I understand or don't understand. Besides, it has nothing to do with me; it's human nature."

"You know my first impression of you was right. You *are* far too sure of yourself."

"No, I've just seen things. That's all."

"You work vice squad?"

"Yeah, for a few months."

"Oh? Any prostitutes in here?"

Hastings examined the surroundings, a slow pan. "No, not yet."

"So when you worked vice, did you roll your jacket sleeves up like Don Johnson?"

"Yeah. When I dropped my car keys in the fish aquarium."

"Don fucking Johnson," she said, slowly emphasizing each word. She'd been drinking. She said, "He always had that stubble on his face. You, you look like you shave every day. Did you ever wear a mustache?"

"Never," Hastings said. "But there were plenty of weekends I didn't shave. There were times I'd go days without shaving."

"How bold of you. How existential."

"Do you want to hear about it?"

"Hear about you not shaving?" She gave him another mock sigh. "Sure," she said.

"I used to go hunting. A lot. And I was very serious about it. Before the hunting trip began, I'd go two, sometimes three days without bathing. I'd brush my teeth, but that was about it."

"That's disgusting."

"No, it was necessary. You have a dog?"

"No. I have a cat though."

"Oh, a cat, that's marvelous," Hastings said. "Well, any dog owner usually has a story about his dog rolling over something that died. Sometimes it's a dead snake. The smell is unholy. A mutt will do it, a show poodle will do it. Do you know why the dog does that?"

"Tell me, o wise man of Nebraska."

"Because every dog is a descendant of a wolf. They're all wolves deep down. And the wolf did that. Any predatory hunting animal will do that before he goes hunting, before he goes after the deer or the rabbit. So the prey doesn't smell him coming."

"But you're a man, not a wolf. You do understand that, don't you?"

"The deer doesn't care. The deer smells soap, he knows it's a man and he's going to run when he smells it."

"You really used to do that?"

"Yeah."

She said, "You still do that?"

"No," Hastings said. "I quit a few years ago. After I got married, with the family, I didn't have the time anymore."

"You miss it?"

"No, not really."

She said, "I think I understand why."

Hastings smiled at that, but let it go.

Carol smiled back at him and there was a moment between them. Which held, briefly among the music and smoke and the smell of whiskey.

Carol said, "I don't know . . ."

He was reasonably sure he understood what she meant by that.

He said, "What don't you know?"

"About this." She said, "I'm not trying to speak out of turn, but . . . I think you're still in love with your wife."

"She's my ex-wife."

"I know," Carol said. "But I'm not sure you've come to terms with that yet."

"Hey —"

"I'm sorry. I didn't mean to get heavy all of a sudden. It's just that —" She stopped herself. Smiled. "Don't worry, we're not going to have one of these relationship conversations. I hate those."

"Okay."

"But I want you to call me in a couple of days," she said.

"Okay."

"If it's what you want to do."

Hastings walked her to her car. Standing in the parking lot in the shadow of the massive Amoco sign off McCausland Avenue.

223

"You okay to drive?" he said.

"I'm good," she said. "Besides, I know whose name to drop if I do get pulled over."

"Well," Hastings said, "that's a start."

She smiled and kissed him on the cheek.

"Like I said, far too sure," she said. Then she was in the car and gone.

Twenty-Seven

Dillon had bought a house in an alias's name a few blocks south of Arsenal Street. It was a small, modest, brick house with a narrow yard and a separate garage in the alley, one of many such houses on many such blocks in the neighborhood. Dillon liked money, liked demanding it, getting it, keeping it, and gathering it. But he had never been tempted to buy anything resembling an estate. And he had never bought a foreign car.

He sat at his kitchen table in his house and tipped a bottle of wine into Frank's glass, then his own.

Frank Cahalin started to lift the glass.

Dillon raised his hand. "Hey," he said, "you know better than that. Let it sit for a minute. Let it breathe."

"Yeah, I know."

Dillon regarded the younger man. Frank was only a few years younger than him, but he had always thought of him as sort of a son. He had once reminded Frank that they had met many years before Frankie became an FBI agent. Specifically, that Frank had come into an Irish pub in Chicago's Bridgeport neighborhood with his mom and dad when he was maybe ten years old and Dillon had been there meeting with the then-feared gangster Jerry Doyle. Dillon, then eighteen, already looking like he was about thirty; Dillon being one of those creatures that seems to jump over adolescence to manhood and is never, ever referred to as "kid." Frank had said, yeah, he remembered, looking uncomfortable. And Dillon had known why. Frank's dad had been a boozer and had never amounted to anything and he had probably been hammered that day. Even back then, everyone knew Dillon. He was a respected man. Frank was at the age where he starting to become aware that his old man was an embarrassment. His dad was older than Dillon then. But Frank remembered the way his dad had been around Mike Dillon: subdued, respectful, scared, his hands shaking. Dillon had seen young Frank, seen the mild anguish. Dillon nodded at young Frank then, almost smiled. A sympathetic gesture from Mike Dillon on that bleak day was not something Frank would forget.

In his early thirties, Frank Cahalin was an ambitious special agent who had already formed a mind-set not unusual to FBI agents assigned to organized crime. That is, a belief that the Bureau was less a law enforcement agency than it was a sort of government spy ring. To gather intelligence against Mafia figures, alliances were formed with other gangsters, often members of the Mafia themselves. People like Agent Cahalin persuaded themselves that their informants were small-timers, not the menaces to society that John Zanatelli was. Some in the FBI worried that Cahalin had not left his south Chicago admiration for Irish mobsters behind, but they had been in the minority. In any event, Cahalin was encouraged by his superiors to contact Dillon and try to persuade him to start helping his friends in law enforcement.

So Cahalin had.

That had been twelve years ago.

In that time, a sort of bond had formed between the two men. At least, from Frank's perspective it had. Dillon and Jimmy Rizza, who was half Irish, would have Frank over for dinner. They talked and laughed and knocked back a lot of wine. They shared stories of what tough, stubborn people the Irish were; *joked* about the obstinacy of their people. What proud, hard-shelled mother-fuckers they were. Frank became enamored. To him, Mike Dillon was an affable rascal. A man who had done hard time and had learned his lessons and was good to his mother. Dillon took to telling Frank, "You ever need anything, you let me know. Anytime, okay?"

Six years ago, Frank got involved with a girl in his office. She was younger than him. Her name was Darlene and she had been a pom-pom girl for Ohio State University. She was a good fifty pounds lighter than Frank's wife. They would get together at hotel rooms twice a week. This along with gifts and frequent dinners took its toll on the agent's salary. Frank was sent to Miami by the Bureau for a five-day conference. He missed Darlene and he wanted her to come down and spend the weekend with him. But a last-minute flight was about eleven hundred dollars, and he would need another grand for gifts and entertainment once she got there.

Frank called Mike.

Mike said, "I'll take care of it."

That afternoon, Jimmy Rizza brought Darlene an envelope with three thousand dollars in it. That evening, she was on a flight.

Looking at it realistically, there was no going back after that. A few months later, Frank's wife filed for divorce. There was a celebratory dinner at Mike's. As Frank was leaving, Mike said, "Wait a minute," and handed Frank a case of what had become his favorite wine. When Frank got home, he found an envelope under the bottles. There was eight thousand dollars in it. Frank kept it, though he never said anything about it to anyone.

Now, Dillon said, "You worry too much."

Frank said, "You blame me?"

"Look, you just told me they don't know anything. They're looking into some guy who's in Marion, for Christ's sake. Me, I don't even live here."

"You've been living here for two years."

"Yeah, but underground. Who knows I'm here besides you?"

"Jimmy knows. The woman knows."

"So what?"

Frank said, "I still think it'd be better if the both of you left town."

"Leave town? How long should I leave town?"

"Until this situation cools down."

"Frank, it has cooled down. Forty-eight

hours have come and gone and they got nothing. Besides, I don't want to leave."

"Come on, Mike."

"No, you come on. I spent a year driving around this country. Going to small towns and hotels. Country music . . . Jesus. I want to eat good food in nice restaurants. I live on the road, it's like I'm doing time."

"It's better than doing time, Mike."

"Well, I'm not doing that either. Frank, two things I told myself when I came out of prison: one, I was never, ever going back and, two, I was going to live my life the way I want to live it. I've kept that promise. I wouldn't have had to leave Chicago if you'd kept yours."

Frank Cahalin frowned. "What are you talking about?"

"You know goddamn well what I'm talking about."

"Aw come on, Mike. The feds didn't issue a warrant for your arrest. That was state police."

"You said you'd protect me. You gave me your word."

"And I kept it. I can't control what some other law enforcement agency does."

"You could have stayed on top of it. Whatever information they had, it was available to you. It was available."

"Mike, I don't know what you want from me. Don't you think I did the best I could?"

Dillon sighed. "Yeah, I suppose you did." He poured more wine into Frank's glass. "Just don't ask me to leave town, okay? I'm through doing that shit."

"Okay, Mike."

Dillon looked at him again.

Frank Cahalin, Catholic boy in his forties, all tangled up in sin. Frank was getting heavy now and it was showing in his face. Jimmy had once said that Frank looked a little like that statue in front of the restaurant, yeah, Kip's Big Boy, but Dillon got fierce with Jimmy and told him not to show disrespect because Frank was all right.

He remembered the day after they whacked the asshole cop and his partner. Frank had come charging down to Jimmy's garage, almost weeping with rage. Stomping his feet and shouting, but at the end of the day powerless to do anything about it.

Frank had said, "What did I say to you in Chicago? Years ago, what did I tell you?"

Dillon had said, "Ah, come on, Frank."

"What did I say to you?"

"I remember what you said."

"I said you can do what you want, so long as you don't clip anyone. You remember that?"

231

Yeah, Dillon remembered. He had said a lot of things to a lot of people. But the cop had gotten too close. He was on the verge of discovering wanted fugitive Mike Dillon. And if Mike Dillon was caught, it would be the end of Frank Cahalin.

And that was the thing about Frank. He *understood* all of it. Frank knew as well as anybody that the cop had to be clipped. But as Dillon told Jimmy after Frank left, "He knows it had to be done. Deep down, he's relieved it's done. And he feels ashamed that he's relieved. So he needed to come here and yell at us for being bad little boys so he can feel better about it. It doesn't change anything."

Now Dillon said, "Frank, let's not talk about it anymore. Bygones." Dillon's voice was gentler now. "Have some more wine."

TWENTY-EIGHT

They only used half of the gymnasium for the second grade girls' basketball games because it would be too much for the kids to run the entire length of the court. Little girls running chaotically up and down the width of one-half of the court, shooting baskets without aiming. Lee Dunphy was shorter than most of the other girls and not much of a shooter herself, but she hustled and blocked and passed and was valuable to her team.

Sharon sat with the other parents on one of the unfolded chairs they had provided. Mothers yelling as loud as the dads who were there, shouting out directions to their children who couldn't hear them.

There were two coaches for Lee's team. One was a heavyset man who seemed to forget that he was coaching seven-year-old girls. Not a bad guy, but too serious. The second coach was Terry Ross. "Mr. Ross," as Lee called him, was a natural with children. Gentle and kind, yet strong enough and wise enough to know when to tell a girl she was more scared than she was hurt. He had a daughter on the team too — Katie Ross.

It was around the second or third game of the season that Sharon found herself watching Mr. Ross almost as much as she did Lee. He was a good-looking man. She had overheard one of the mothers say he was a widower and an engineer and half the basketball moms were in love with him. Sharon would remind herself that she was plain and even if most of the others weren't married, Terry Ross would surely pick any of them over her. And when Terry began talking to her after games and then before games, she reminded herself that he wasn't really interested in her, but was a decent person who was nice to everyone. It didn't *mean* anything, she thought, in spite of the juvenile knowing glances the other moms gave her.

Halfway through the season, Terry asked Sharon if she and Lee would join him and his daughter for some ice cream. Sharon said yes and then was genuinely surprised to find that it had been an exclusive invite. No other moms, no other children. A pleasant hour quickly passed by as they talked about basketball and kids. They did it a couple more times after that. And it got so that Sharon Dunphy became angry with herself. She wanted to tell this man that she was not normal. That a normal, happy family life was not something she deserved or was meant for. That she felt like a liar and a fraud even as she enjoyed the time she spent with him. That they could not be husband and wife and raise his daughter and her two children together.

Tonight, when the game ended, Terry came over with Lee walking alongside him. God, Sharon thought, he doesn't make it easy. The two of them looking natural together. The first possible decent father figure in Lee's life, and it was not meant to be.

"Hey," Terry said.

"Hey." To Lee, Sharon said, "You did great, honey."

Sharon said other encouraging words to her daughter before the little girl ran off to talk with her friends, and then Sharon was left alone with the man she had fallen in love with.

Terry Ross said, "Can I sit?"

"Sure."

Sharon was aware of the other moms

watching him. They think we're dating now, she thought. Courting. The body language, the smiles. People could think they were married.

Terry Ross said, "I thought maybe we could have some dinner."

Sharon said, "Tonight?"

"No," he said. "I meant, this weekend. I mean, just the two of us."

She looked at him, a slight pain on her face.

She said, "Let's talk about it outside."

Terry Ross looked away. "Well . . . perhaps some other time." Being gracious now; he was the sort of man that would not bother her if she did not want to be bothered.

"I don't think you understand," Sharon said. "Walk with me."

In the school parking lot, they put their children in their respective cars and spoke on the lot in lowered voices.

Sharon said, "I can't get involved with you."

He said, "Okay. Well, I understand."

"No, you don't understand. You really don't understand." Sharon said, "I like you very much. I'd like to see you and get to know you better. But it's not going to work. There are things you don't know about me."

"I know what I need to know. I know you're a good mother and that you're a very nice person." He said, "I think you know how I feel about you."

"Please don't say things like that."

"Why not? It's the truth."

"It can't work. I'm not meant to — do you know about my ex-husband?"

"I've been told."

Sharon was not surprised. One of the other mothers had found some way of letting him know. Women were often the worst enemies of women. Sharon smiled with some bitterness. "Yes," she said, "I suppose you have."

"I know he's in prison," Terry Ross said. "I don't care. You're the one I like."

"Do you know what you're doing?"

"I know exactly what I'm doing."

"No," she said, "you don't. Terry, it's . . . too late for me to have — this. I need you to understand that."

"Listen, if you're not interested —"

"No, that's not it at all." She took his hand. "Not at all."

"Then what?"

"I can't explain it to you. Just trust me, okay." She released his hand. "You deserve something better. Find another girl. A nice girl who can be your wife and a good mother to Katie. Forget about me."

"But I've already found a nice girl."

"No, you haven't."

Terry stepped in and put his hands on her arms. "I have," he said and kissed her.

She kissed him back and for a moment stopped thinking and let it become passionate. For a moment, she wished she were in an alternate universe or life where this could continue and they could eat together and rent movies together and be lovers and husband and wife and mother and father. But then she remembered that it could only be a fantasy and she pushed him back.

"Don't do that again," she said, her voice shaking. "Please."

She hurried to her car, leaving him standing alone in the parking lot.

A few minutes after they both drove their vehicles off the lot, the lights of a black Pontiac, parked on the other side, came on as its engine started. Dillon shifted the car into gear and drove away.

Twenty-Nine

Dillon met May Connelly at a party at Jerry Doyle's house a couple of years after he got out of prison. Blonde and long-legged, she was the kind of girl he had thought about when he was locked up. A magazine girl come to life. She told him that she admired Princess Diana and that her favorite movie was *Grease.* He set her up in an apartment on the Gold Coast and gave her a black Trans Am. She was twenty-three when he met her.

When she was twenty-eight, he found out she was running around with another guy. A car salesman. When he confronted her about it, she admitted it and told him that he, Dillon, was a great guy, but she wanted to start a new life. Maybe the car salesman would marry her, maybe he wouldn't, but she thought it was best that she and Dillon stop seeing each other.

Dillon said she should do whatever made

239

her happy.

The next night, he took May Connelly to his house and strangled her to death. With Jimmy's help, they buried her in the northern woods of Wisconsin.

Jimmy Rizza had never asked Dillon to explain why they were doing this. Dillon told Jimmy that May was planning to leave him. That was enough.

On this night, Dillon had seen Sharon kiss another man. Just some yutz driving a Dodge minivan. What was that? What was wrong with her? Dillon had never told her about killing the deputy, never spoke of it aloud. But she had to have known he was involved in it. She wasn't dumb. Having known about that, why would she run around with this piece of shit?

No, she was not dumb. Just ungrateful. He paid her mortgage and helped her out and she was fooling around with some cluck driving a minivan. At least May had been honest about things, had admitted what she was doing and told him she was going to leave him.

Although, that in itself offended Dillon. The idea that May could just *tell* him it was over. Like she was the one in control. Stupid bitch. Stupid ungrateful whore. Sharon, in contrast, was lying to him. Again. Keeping things from him. Again. Betraying him.

Well.

It would have to be done now. She would have to be killed and made to disappear. And the kids too. The kids had seen him at the house. There was no way around it. He'd feel better if they were all in Chicago. The northern woods of Wisconsin were a short drive from there. It would be a long drive from here. He and Jimmy would have to take turns at the wheel.

THIRTY

There were three black and white county patrol cars and one highway patrol cruiser at the IHOP on Lindbergh Boulevard. A common "Signal 13" for law enforcement. Lunch.

Deputy Damon Jacobs was sitting inside with other deputies among plates with oversized portions and buttered toast. The uniformed deputies regarded the plainclothes detectives as they approached the table. Obligatory handshakes were exchanged and then Jacobs walked to another table with Hastings and Murph.

Damon Jacobs said, "What can I do for you?"

Hastings said, "It's my understanding you were a close friend of Chris Hummel's."

"That's right. I was best man at his wedding. And we went through academy together."

Hastings said, "What was your personal

impression of him?"

Damon Jacobs said, "What do you mean?"

"I think you know what I mean."

"He was a good officer," Jacobs said. "Conscientious, smart . . . honest. You hearing something different?"

"Yeah," Hastings said. "From the people he put in jail. But I want to know what you think."

The deputy looked at the detectives one at a time, then looked back at Hastings. "What is this?" he said.

Murph said, "We're not here to trash him. We're homicide, okay. Not I.A. We're trying to find out if there was some personal reason someone had for killing him."

Deputy Jacobs said, "Personal? I'd say he took it very personally."

Hastings said, "You want to help us or not?"

Jacobs said, "Okay. I already told you: Chris Hummel was clean. He did not steal. He did not take freebies. That doesn't mean he was perfect. But he was a clean cop."

Hastings said, "What do you mean?"

"I mean, he was immature. He took a while to grow up." Jacobs said, "You how know how young cops are."

Murph said, "You mean he was fucking around on his wife."

"Yeah."

Hastings said, "Who with?"

"Aww, there were a lot of girls. There was a girl who worked in dispatch. Tracy something or other. . . . Walsh. Tracy Walsh. There was a probation and parole officer. Her name was Brama or Ramma or something. There was a nurse he used to see when he worked security at the hospital."

Hastings said, "Do you remember her name?"

Deputy Jacobs signaled to another deputy. He came over to the table. His identification strip on his pocket said his name was Fuchs.

"Roy," Jacobs said. "Who was that nurse Chris used to run around with, worked at Southcrest?"

"You mean Trudy?"

"Yeah, that's it. Trudy. She still at Southcrest?"

"Last I heard."

Hastings said, "Trudy what?"

The deputies sought answers in each other's expressions until one said "West" and the other one said, "Yeah, Trudy West."

There was a smile on Roy Fuchs's face when he hit the name, and it was not lost on Hastings.

Hastings said to the deputies, "This Trudy

West, she been with other cops?"

Jacobs waited until Fuchs left and spoke in a different tone to the detectives.

"Yeah, but . . . hey," he said, "I want to make it clear that Chris stopped the running around over a year ago. He really did. His old lady actually filed divorce papers on him and he went to her on his knees, literally, and begged her to take him back. And she did. Now you can call him a pussy for doing that, but I wouldn't."

Hastings said, "She took him back?"

"Yeah. Last year. Listen," Jacobs said, "the man just spent over forty thousand dollars fixing up their house. Would a man do that if he was planning to leave his wife?"

"He might," Murph said.

"Well," Jacobs said, "he wasn't."

"Okay," Hastings said. He motioned to Murph that they were finished. They stood and Hastings said to the deputy, "How did you know Hummel was paying to have his house redecorated? Did he tell you?"

Jacobs said, "He told everybody."

In the car, Murph said, "So the man ran around on his wife. So fucking what?"

Hastings turned to regard the man. He said, "You mad at me, Murph?"

"No, I'm not mad at you. I just don't like

this. This gets out and it embarrasses him, his family. What does it have to do with anything?"

"It might have plenty to do with it. We keep checking for things related to the man's work, but we can't ignore the personal. You know that."

"So two cops get machine-gunned because one of them can't keep his pants on?"

"I don't know. Maybe he banged the wrong girl. An angry boyfriend. Or husband."

"Machine guns, George. That was a professional hit."

"Then maybe it was a professional's girlfriend."

"Maybe," Murph said. Though he didn't seem too sure about it.

"Hey," Hastings said, "did you ever hear about that Tulsa homicide with the bow and arrow?"

"No."

"This cop's wife was divorcing him, sleeping with another guy. So he decided to kill her. While he was on duty, he crept to her window and killed her with a bow and arrow."

"A bow and arrow?"

"Yeah. He was a hunter, apparently."

"Fucking barbarian. Why didn't he just

use a gun?"

"I don't know," Hastings said. "Guess he wanted to use the bow and arrow. It's a silent weapon. Anyway, like I said, the dumbass did this while he was on break while on duty. So he's gone for half an hour. His partner got questioned and . . ."

"Wouldn't cover for him?"

"He covered for him. For about a day. But then caved after they leaned on him, or got a good lawyer, and said, no, he could not account for his partner's whereabouts for at least thirty minutes."

"So they got him?"

"Yeah, they got him."

Hastings waited for a light to change from red to green. When it did, he moved the Jag forward and shifted over to the right lane to take the entrance ramp to I-64.

"Okay," Murph said, "what's the point?"

"I don't know," Hastings said, "I was just thinking about it."

"That a cop can go bad? Is that the point?"

"No," Hastings said. "The point is that everyone has a secret life. Or another life. The one outside of work that we think we know, but we don't. That cop in Tulsa, he was working in law enforcement and he wanted to impale the mother of his children with an arrow, for Christ's sake. I'll bet no one he worked with thought he was capable of that."

"I wouldn't be too sure of that. That partner of his may have been wise."

Hastings shrugged. He said, "I want you and Rhodes to examine what Hummel was doing the week before this shooting."

"You mean off duty?"

"No. On duty. Get the dispatch logs and the tapes of the radio calls. Check them thoroughly. I want to know every place those guys went and when."

"You mean, while on duty?"

"Yeah."

"Okay," Murph said. They rode in silence for a while.

And Murph said, "You're going to talk to these women Jacobs told you about it?"

"All three," Hastings said. "Kind of like *The Dating Game.*"

"Well," Murph said, "you should interview them separately, though."

Hastings looked at the detective for four seconds before saying, "Yeah, okay."

THIRTY-ONE

At a station north of Springfield, Illinois, Regan used cash to pay for the gasoline. He was driving a light blue Mercury Marquis. He started the car, let the engine settle as he hesitated for a moment. He drove the car to the side of the building where the convenience store employees parked. He stopped the car there and put it in park and leaned back and closed his eyes.

He had not slept since leaving Max Collins's house the night before. It had taken him that long to line up the car and traveling money and new weapons. When he was younger, he would take speed to keep himself awake. Whiskey later to come down. Ping-pong. He had stopped doing that, had learned to listen to his body when it told him he needed to sleep.

He closed his eyes and thought of Mike Dillon. A job in Louisville. One of Mike's friends had partnered with a businessman.

Big Barney's Car Wash. Though the guy in Louisville was named Barry, not Barney. He liked Big Barney better, he said. Though Dillon had said the guy thought his own name sounded too Jewish. Barry Donfin, that had been the guy's name. Dillon said Barry had been taking more than his share of the profits. Or hiding things. Or maybe Barry Donfin had just rubbed Dillon the wrong way. Dillon could be like that. He had once killed a guy because the guy kept calling him "Rex." Jimmy Rizza told Regan the guy should have known better, which explained nothing. Regan took half of Dillon's forty thousand and drove to Louisville through the night. He waited in the parking lot of a country club for Barry Donfin to come out. Waited until Barry bent over the trunk of a beige Cadillac to put his golf clubs in, then shot Barry three times with a high-powered rifle.

He was off the parking lot seconds after Barry slumped to the ground. Easy. Returned to Chicago and picked up the rest of his fee from Dillon.

No. Regan had never had any personal trouble with Dillon.

Or Jimmy Rizza, for that matter. It would not be accurate to say they were friends. They knew each other, grew up in circumstances not dissimilar. To the degree nature allowed, they even understood each other. There were differences between them, and Regan liked to think he recognized those differences. Jack Regan was, too, a born killer. But he was selective and he was careful. He was good at killing, but he did not do it without purpose. He would not kill someone for calling him a mick or a faggot or a piece of shit or "Rex." For Dillon and Rizza, the insults and double crosses gave them an opportunity to let blood flow. And where these opportunities did not exist, they could be very imaginative in creating them.

Regan regretted that Jimmy had sent his brother after him. It meant that Regan had no choice but to kill not only Sean but, now, Jimmy as well. He had planned to simply meet with Jimmy and ask him where Dillon was. He had little doubt that Jimmy would know this. And he had also believed that Jimmy would not hesitate to give up Mike. Irish, Italian, Russian . . . whatever. All these guys eventually ratted each other out. The Italian pricking of fingers and sharing of blood and the Irishman's talk of Dublin and the famine and the year God forgot Ireland, it was all silly. Human nature was human nature and blarney was blarney and brothers were brothers. Jimmy would know by now that Regan had killed Sean and there was nothing that was going to change that. Jimmy would now want to kill him and there would be no reasoning with him.

None of this bothered Regan on any personal level. To his way of thinking, it was Jimmy who had crossed the line, Jimmy who had brought his brother into it.

Ah, Regan thought, forget these things. For now.

He opened his eyes and closed them again and concentrated on the sound of trucks rolling by in the distance. Within minutes he was asleep.

THIRTY-TWO

Senior probation and parole officer Brahma Jones asked if he was going to read her the Garrity warning.

Hastings said, "Garrity? This isn't a disciplinary investigation."

Brahma Jones said, "It's not, huh?"

And Hastings saw it coming.

"No," he said, "it's not."

Brahma Jones said, "Then I ain't got a fucking thing to say to you."

She was a short, heavy woman, a roll of tummy hanging over her belt. Chris Hummel had been skinny. Hastings looked at her and an unpleasant image of the two of them formed in his mind, and he quickly escorted it to the door.

They were in the break room of the local probationary office, Hastings sitting at a table with this woman who was getting tough with him for some reason.

Hastings said, "What are you concerned about?"

The woman said, "First of all, I'm married."

Hastings shrugged. "Hummel was married too."

"You're missing the point," she said. "I don't fool around."

"Officer," Hastings said, "this is a criminal investigation. You are not the target of this investigation. You want to plead the fifth even though you're only a witness, I can't stop you. But if you do that, I'll go straight to your supervisor and tell him you refused to cooperate with me on a murder investigation of a brother officer. And I'll back it up with a letter that I will insist be placed in your personnel file. Now if you tell me that nothing was going on and it's true, then we're done and you have my apologies. But if you lie to me, even once, I will hammer you."

The woman stared at him, not having the strength to show anger.

"It's not your business," she said.

"If it relates to his murder, it's very much my business."

"It doesn't relate to it. Not one bit."

"I'll make that determination, officer. Are we clear?"

"I —"

"Are we clear?"

"Yes. *Lieutenant.*" She stated his rank like it was something you step on.

Hastings said, "Let me say for the record, I don't give a shit if you slept with him in his mother's bed. I'm not here to judge you. And this is not an internal affairs investigation. But — people saw you together. And they formed impressions about it." He said, "Were those impressions wrong?"

"I'm married," she said.

"Were those impressions wrong?"

The woman looked away from him. "No," she said, "they're not wrong."

Hastings eased back, a little. He said, "Did your husband know?"

"No."

"Are you absolutely sure of that?"

"Yes. I'm absolutely sure of that."

"I understand your husband works for St. Charles PD. Correct?"

"Yes."

"Do you know where he was the night of the murders?"

"He was on duty. In St. Charles. It's miles away."

"Okay," Hastings said. "And you?"

"I was doing home visits to offenders. It's in my logs. You want to question the people

I visited, go ahead."

"Okay."

After a moment, Brahma Jones said, "You don't actually think I killed him, do you?"

"No. I just need to check things off."

The woman said, "Man, you are reaching."

She was trying to get something back now because he had threatened her. Hastings ignored it. He said, "What did you think of Chris?"

"What do you mean?"

"I mean, was he nice, was he cruel? Did he ever scare you or hurt you?"

"He was fun is what he was." She said, "No. He never hurt me or scared me. That's not the kind of man he was. He was actually very nice." The woman was looking at him. "Whose side are you on?"

"His."

"Yeah, well," she said, "he was a good officer. And he was not the sort to rough women up. I promise you that." Her voice broke toward the end.

Shit, Hastings thought. He felt ashamed. He put that aside too and said, "How did it end with you two?"

"It just fizzled out. I know Chris. I was well aware that I wasn't the first and I wouldn't be the last."

"So he moved on."

"Yes," she said. "To some other lonely, fat girl. But I'm not sorry for what we did. You can write that down if you want."

"That's all right," Hastings said. "You say he moved on; you mean to another woman or back to his wife?"

"Probably another woman."

"Okay. How did you feel when you found out he had been killed?"

"What do you think?"

Hastings remembered sitting at a trial and watching a shrewd defense lawyer cross-examining a sad old lady in a quiet, patient tone, asking the woman if she took medication for mental illness and she answered that yes, she did and the lawyer took his sweet time and made her list every sort of pill she had ingested. After each one, the lawyer would say, "And what else?" until tears started rolling down the old lady's face. The prosecutor objected to the cruel line of questioning, and the defense lawyer told the judge he was by no means enjoying this, but that it was necessary on the issue of credibility. The lawyer was slick enough that Hastings almost believed it. In any event, the man had to do his job.

Hastings said, "Do you want to answer my question?"

"I felt like shit." Brahma Jones said, "Happy now?"

"No," Hastings said. "One more thing. Was he clean?"

Brahma Jones strengthened her lower chin. She said, "He was the cleanest cop I've ever met." And everything about her expression at that moment said, *Cleaner and better and nicer than you, Detective. A better man than you.*

Later, she walked out of the break room. Murph, who had been waiting in the hall on Hastings's instructions, stepped back against a vending machine, gave a mock leer to her hind end after she walked past him. It made Hastings feel worse.

Hastings walked up next to Murph.

Murph said, "Well?"

"She's okay," Hastings said.

"So you're eliminating her as a suspect?"

"Probably."

Murph said, "Did they — ?"

"Yeah. She was in love with him."

"Hmmm," Murph said. "Ready for the next one?"

"Can't wait," Hastings said.

Deputy Connie Birdsong was in full uniform when they interviewed her — tan slacks, dark brown tunic. They sat at a small table in an interview room at the county headquarters. She was a tall woman with broad shoulders and a short, unfashionable haircut, and she sat in her chair the way a man would. They had barely started their questions when she burst into tears.

Hastings wasn't ready for this at all. Murph had his mouth slightly open, mildly shocked. She was an officer in uniform wearing OC spray, ammunition clips, and a fully loaded weapon on her side. But here she was weeping like Tonya Harding over a broken shoestring.

Hastings said, "There's nothing to be upset about."

She said, "Am I going to lose my job?"

"No, we're just —"

"I can't lose my job —"

"That's not going to —"

"— I didn't do anything —"

"Connie," Hastings said, "Connie. Will you please calm down?"

Deputy Connie Birdsong drew a few breaths. She steadied herself, bit by bit, resting her hands on her knees.

Hastings said, "Okay?"

"Okay," she said.

Hastings said, "Now, I don't want you to take this the wrong way. But we have information you were having an affair with Chris

Hummel. Is that true?"

Connie Birdsong nodded. Her mouth closed, as she struggled to hold back the tears.

Hastings said, "It is true?"

"Yes."

"When was it?"

"About two years ago."

"You were married too, correct?"

"Yes, sir."

"Did your husband ever find out?"

"Yes. Yes, sir."

"How did he find out?"

"I told him."

Murph said, "You told him?"

"Yes, sir."

Murph said, "Why?"

"I told my minister. At church. He said that's what I should do." Deputy Birdsong said, "I told my husband and then I told the congregation at the church. It's what Ben said I should do."

Hastings said, "I thought your husband's name was Martin?"

"It is," she said. "Ben is our minister."

Murph said, "Your minister made you tell everyone at church?"

"Yes, sir."

Murph said, "What church is this?"

The question seemed to wound the

woman. It was her religion they were messing with now.

She said to Murph, "What church do *you* go to?"

"Never mind that," Hastings said. "About how many people are in this congregation?"

"Around fifty," she said. "It's a small church." She added, "But we like it."

Hastings said, "When did you make this confession?"

"It was about a year and a half ago."

Hastings looked at Murph and Murph looked back at him. Hastings said, "Did you feel better after you made the confession?"

"Definitely."

Murph said, "How about your husband? Did he feel better?"

"Yes. We worked through it."

Hastings said, "Your husband works at Boeing, correct?"

"Yes, sir. He's an aerospace engineer."

Hastings said, "Where was he the night Chris Hummel was killed?"

Deputy Birdsong counted back the days. She reached it, then said, "He was with me. We were at church, getting ready for a bake sale."

Murph said, "I believe it."

Hastings gave him a look and said, "Can you give us names and numbers of people who saw you there?"

"Oh, yes, sir."

The detectives looked at each other again, seeing if the other had something else to say.

Deputy Birdsong said, "I'm not going to lose my job, am I?"

Hastings said, "For what?"

"For — you know."

Hastings said, "I strongly doubt it."

And Murph said, "Lady, they start firing police officers for that, they're not going to have the manpower left to patrol Tower Grove Park."

Hastings waited for a county patrol car to pull into the parking lot before he drove the Jaguar out into the street.

Murph said, "Are you Catholic?"

"No," Hastings said. "You?"

"Yeah." Murph said, "We have confession too. It's not like that, though. It's to a priest. When I was a kid, the priest'd be behind a screen so you couldn't see him. I went last year, before Easter Sunday, though, and then you just sat in front of him in front of the whole church."

"So now it's like what she did?"

"No. No one hears what you're saying. Except the priest. It's just that people who are waiting in line can see you. The priest, he hears you." Murph said, "Still, I liked it better the old way."

"Protestants think that's wrong too, don't they?"

"What, confessing your sins to a priest?"

Hastings was thinking of his father. The man could quote New Testament passages chapter and verse. A Protestant of the John Knox school, Carl Hastings hated Catholics. When Hastings was a teenager, he finally figured out that dad was a man full of resentment and anger and meanness of spirit. A small man who probably despised his son and wife for seeing through him. In one of their last conversations before Hastings had left for St. Louis, he had heard his father say something vicious to his mother, something ugly enough to send her from the kitchen in tears. Hastings said to the old man, "You're not even interested in religion. You just want to carve people up and claim that it's for the greater glory of God." He waited for the old man to make his move, so he could have an excuse to belt him. But Carl was a man of violent words, not action, and a coward, so he kept still. In the solitary years that followed, Hastings more or less came to terms with the fact that he had been a miserable creep. He believed that if there was a hell and he went there, he would probably meet up with Carl on a talk show set, with Jerry Springer or some other demon trying to coax a bogus reconciliation between them before the inevitable exchange of swinging chairs.

"Yeah," Hastings said. He wished he hadn't said anything about priests now.

But Murph only shrugged. "Beats saying it to a church full of people," he said. Murph looked out the window. Hastings hoped Murph would not start waxing philosophical about the nature of sin and redemption and congregants wondering if Connie Birdsong was game for another round.

Murph was shaking his head now. He said, "Can you believe her crying like that?"

Hastings smiled. He shrugged. He sensed the onset of a conversation he did not want to have.

Murph said, "I mean, come on. She's a police officer, for God's sake."

Hastings said, "She's not typical."

"Yeah, I know, but goddamn. That interview was nothing. How does she handle things when they really get hot?"

"Murph, I really don't —"

"You know what the problem is?"

"No."

"Lieutenant, you know I don't have issues with women cops. I mean, I hope you know that. But if a man in uniform behaved that way, we both know they'd get rid of him."

Hastings thought of Marvin Tate. The relief he felt when Marvin resigned.

"Maybe," Hastings said.

"But she gets to stay. And I bet I know why. I'll bet she's got a supervisor who's afraid of disciplining her because he's afraid he'll get sued. Or, she'll file a complaint on him and fuck up his career. Or, he's one of those supervisors who *looks out* for her, treats her like the little girl he never had. Or he's hoping one day she'll give him a piece himself."

"Yeah, maybe."

"But other officers got to work with her. They'll need her to back them up. And then what happens?"

"Murph."

"At the end of the day, it's a failure of leadership. You know what I mean?"

"Murph."

"Yeah?"

"Another time, okay?"

"Yeah, okay."

"Let's talk about the investigation. Did you call Rhodes about the dispatch logs?"

"Yeah. Rhodes asked if we should get

Hummel's cell phone records too. I agreed it was a good idea."

"Good. Yeah, that is a good idea."

"We were going to go over them this evening."

"Okay. I'm going to run you back to the station. Then I'll drive out to interview the nurse."

In the early days of their courtship, Hastings and Eileen had had the conversation that women and men the world over have had. The man charges that a woman can have sex anytime she wants while a man cannot. Eileen responded that men could have sex anytime they wanted as well. Eileen said George could go to a bar on any given night and bring a woman home to his bed and that he may not like how the woman looked or talked or how much she drank, but he could find one if he wanted. Eileen could not be persuaded otherwise.

It was one of those silly arguments they had with drinks and cigarettes that neither one cared to win so long as it gave them something to laugh about and engage with each other over, back when they cared about each other enough to do it.

But Hastings thought about it when he met with Trudy West, R.N., at Southcrest

Hospital.

Like Connie Birdsong and Brahma Jones, Trudy West was unattractive. There was no getting away from it. Hastings told himself that it had nothing to do with the case. He told himself that it was not his place to judge the slain police officer. Not over something like this. He wondered if the women looked like they could have appeared in *Sports Illustrated* swimsuit issues, would he feel the same way? Would he feel not sadness, but perhaps envy and admiration? All right, Hummel. Go team. Shit. It was adultery either way. When Eileen had been unfaithful, he did not stop to wonder if the other fellow was handsome or ugly.

Why should it make any difference? If Hummel sought out lonely, unattractive women to seduce, what should it matter? There seemed to be no evidence that he mistreated or abused them. It should only matter if it related to his murder.

Hastings remembered seeing the video footage on national news of the spurned wife in Texas running over her husband with her Lexus. Stopping the car after the first strike and backing over him as he lay struggling to survive. Killing him with most definite premeditation. He remembered seeing a counselor, a woman, interviewed on television saying the lady should not go to prison for the murder . . . the interviewer saying, well, what punishment then? And the woman counselor responding with complete seriousness, "Well, definitely counseling."

Trudy West, wearing light green scrubs, spoke with him in the hallway of the hospital.

She said, "He used to work security here. Nights. That's how we met."

Hastings said, "How long did it go on?"

"A few months. He would call me on his cell phone, sometimes come here on his breaks."

"How come?"

"Well . . . I had breaks too."

Hastings could ask her if he dropped by to chat or if they would sneak off to a broom closet, but he didn't see the point.

He said, "When did it end?"

"Over three years ago."

"How did it end?"

"You mean, was it amicable?"

"Yes."

"Sure it was. He was a nice man. It wasn't just — sex. He would visit my house too. He helped me with my kids. My husband left me several years ago. Chris would come by sometimes and cut my lawn. Come in, have a soda, and leave. He'd do that without asking for anything in return."

"Were you angry with him?"

"Why would I be angry with him?"

"I don't know."

Nurse West shook her head. "He was a kind man. He had flaws, like the rest of us. Yes, he liked to fool around with women. But if you weren't interested in doing that, he was okay with it. He never pushed. And he liked helping people. It's why he became a police officer."

"Did he tell you that?"

"No," she said. "Look, I've been around, okay? I know that when someone makes a big point of telling you the importance of being nice, they're usually not very nice. It's the same with him. He never said he became a police officer because he wanted to help people, but you could see it in how he acted."

"So you liked him?"

"Yeah, I liked him. But . . . that's not the point. Listen, there was a girl that used to work here. She had a neighbor who was a real jerk. He would get drunk and make a lot of noise and say ugly things to her in front of her children. A bully. It made her cry and the police in her neighborhood said they couldn't do anything because he wasn't committing any crimes. Well, he was sure scaring the devil out of her. So I told Chris about it."

"This woman ask you to do that?"

"No. She was just telling me. I made the decision to tell Chris."

"And what did he do?"

"I guess he went over to the neighbor's house and just scared the you-know-what out of him. Told him if he didn't start showing respect for Sharon and her family and the rest of the neighborhood, he was going to come back and, well, I guess beat him up. And you know, I think he would have done it too."

"Did it work?"

"Oh, heck yes. The guy got so scared he eventually moved someplace else." Trudy West reflected for a moment. She said, "I wonder if Chris knew something else about him. Like if he was selling dope or something."

If he didn't, Hastings thought, Hummel could have planted it on him.

Hastings said, "When was this?"

"Oh, this was years ago. When he and I were seeing each other."

She seemed to be studying Hastings now. In a respectful tone, she said, "He was a good man. Not many people would have done what he did."

"I hear you," Hastings said. "Do you remember this neighbor's name?"

"No. No one ever told me that."

"But your friend, this Sharon, she would know, right?"

"I guess she would. But she doesn't work here anymore."

THIRTY-THREE

No one called Jimmy to tell him his brother had been killed. He found out about it by reading it in the *Chicago Sun-Times.* Sean dead, Bacon dead. Max had been killed too; shot to death in his own home. There was no one left to call Jimmy and say, sorry for muffing the job. Sean had been the only family he had left. Jimmy realized that there could well be no one back home who thought he was even alive, so that made him dead too in a way. Two years now of running and living in places he didn't want to live. Running from police and prison and now from Jack Regan.

Jack Regan had killed his brother.

How?

How had Jack pulled that off? Sean was smart, but Jack was smarter. Jimmy should have known. He should have called Sean and told him to bring more guys, to wait for Jack to walk into a parking lot, to stick a bomb under his car, to avoid going into the man's place because the man would know his place better than intruders. He should have gone up to Chicago and done it himself. Maybe taken Mike with him. Though it would have taken a lot of effort to talk Mike into it. Mike Dillon wasn't afraid of anyone, not even Jack Regan, but Mike Dillon wouldn't be dumb enough to return to Chicago. Mike hadn't stayed out of prison by being dumb.

Dillon had called him earlier and said they needed to get rid of Sharon.

Jimmy had said, "Sharon? What are you talking about?"

"It's gotta be done."

"Mike, can you show a little fucking compassion here? I just lost my kid brother."

"I know that, for Christ's sake. We're going to take care of that."

"How are we going to take care of that."

"We'll clip Jack."

"How the fuck we going to do that?" Jimmy had known Jack Regan for a long time. Remote and dangerous, Regan was one of the few people Jimmy Rizza actually feared. "We got three dead men reminding us he's not so easy to kill."

"Christ, Jimmy. He's not a ghost."

"He's coming, Mike."

"All right, all right. But we need to take care of Sharon tonight."

"What's the hurry?"

Dillon said, "No hurry. I just want to get it done."

Now Jimmy waited in his garage for Mike. When he got here they would prepare, then drive over to Sharon's and get it done. Jimmy resigned himself to it. You didn't say no to Mike Dillon. Jimmy remembered a couple who had scrimped and saved and borrowed to buy a tavern in Chicago. And after they did and cleaned it up, Dillon saw its appeal. He approached the couple one evening and said he'd like to take the tavern off their hands. The husband said no thanks. Dillon motioned to Jimmy, and Jimmy took the man's ten-year-old boy by the shoulders. Dillon said, "You see that kid? He's going to be dead tomorrow unless you sign that deed over to me. Understand?" The man signed it over. Dillon gave the owner five thousand for it, telling the guy, "What the hell, we're both Irish, huh?" The five thousand was only a fraction of what the man had borrowed from the bank.

Christ, Jimmy thought. Now they had to go kill some broad and bury her probably because she had put too much butter on Mike's toast or something. Hadn't done it the way Mom used to. Or she had shown interest in another dude, probably a younger one. Typical Mike.

Rhodes said, "County's system is pretty much like ours. Each of their patrol cars has a GPS system, monitors where the cars are at any given time, transmits it back to dispatch. Keeps the patrol officers from going to whorehouses and bars. If dispatch doesn't hear from the officers for a long period of time, they'll do a 10-90. An officer welfare check. Now for the last four months, the proper response has been for the officer to give his unit number. Before that, they were to give the address they were at. If they don't give the proper response, dispatch presumes they're in trouble, maybe being held at gunpoint, and they send backup."

They were in the squad room gathered around Hastings's desk. Murph, Rhodes, Hastings, and Cain.

Hastings said, "In the week before the shootings, were there any 10-90s?"

"There were," Rhodes said. "Just a couple. But the officers only had to give back the unit number."

Hastings said, "Not the address."

"No," Rhodes said.

There was an audible sigh in the room.

"And," Rhodes said, "when the officers went Signal 13 for lunch, they usually said where they were at. But a couple of times they didn't. So we don't know where they were then. They could have been having lunch at Childers's house or Hummel's. Other officers do that sometimes."

By now days had passed since the officers had been massacred. The public leaned on the politicians, the politicians leaned on the chief, the chief leaned on the assistant chief, and so on and so on. They wanted the matter solved. And the officers only had to give back unit numbers.

Hastings said, "You've got the dispatch logs?"

Rhodes said, "Yes."

"You've reviewed them?"

"Yes."

"Anything stand out?"

Rhodes said, "Citations, DUI arrests, a few possession busts. Just standard fare."

"What do you mean?"

Rhodes looked at the other detectives, some uncertainty in his expression. "Well," he said, "what I mean is, we can interview all these people they arrested or gave citations to the week before the shootings. But I'm not sure what good it would do. They've given thousands of citations over the years. Do we interview all them too?"

Hastings sighed. "Yeah, I know what you mean. But let's check them out for the previous week anyway. Maybe someone can give us something."

There was a general feeling of depression in the air about them. They all wanted to solve it, catch the murderers of police officers. And like Hastings they had placed a certain amount of faith in the new technologies, things like GPS tracking systems and tape-recorded dispatches. But all they had learned was that Chris Hummel was a clean cop who liked to get laid. It would have been a whole lot better to have a witness who knew something and saw something.

"Bobby," Hastings said. "I want you to check something out for me. The nurse at the hospital told me that Hummel may have roughed up a neighbor of one of her co-workers. She doesn't know the neighbor's name, but the woman's name was Sharon Dunphy. She used to be a nurse's assistant at Southcrest."

Cain said, "Hummel roughed up this woman's neighbor?"

"Well," Hastings said, "he *may* have. Apparently, Dunphy's neighbor was hassling her and Hummel went over to the guy's house and talked to him."

Cain said, "How long ago was this?"

"Over three years ago."

Bobby Cain frowned.

"Yeah, I know," Hastings said. "Talk to the woman anyway. Find out the ex-neighbor's name and then check him out." He handed a piece of paper to Cain. "Here's her address."

There was a silence in the room that didn't mean anything at first. Then Cain said, "Are you giving up on Treats?"

Hastings looked at Cain. He was aware of the other detectives watching him, waiting for the answer. The distinction between "are *you*" and "are *we*" was not lost on Hastings. He could say "Are you challenging me?" But it probably wouldn't play well. Better to tell the truth.

Hastings said, "I don't know yet." He was not going to say anything else and he looked directly at Cain to see if the man wanted to keep going.

Cain hesitated and then shook his head slightly.

Hastings said, "It's an order, sergeant. Take Murph with you."

Cain said, "Yes, *sir.*" And that wasn't lost on Hastings either. And for a brief moment he had to remind himself not to lose his temper. To resist the urge to tell the sergeant that Murph or even Rhodes deserved the rank more than he did and if he had something to say, say it and put aside this head-shaking chickenshit. Or just ask the little bastard to step outside and take a fucking beating. But he let it pass.

There was another silence after Murph and Cain left. Rhodes seemed to think about his words before he spoke and then he simply said, "I'll start lining up a list of interviews on those citations."

"Okay, Howard. Thanks."

In the hallway, Murph said, "I got to take a leak."

Cain said. "I'll wait in the car." He took the stairs down to the parking lot. He wondered if he should say something to Murphy. Ask him if he agreed with the lieutenant. If he did, the guy would probably side with Hastings. Dumbshit. Whatever the lieutenant says, goes. Like the guy was some sort of fucking Zen master. Stupid, unimaginative clucks, all of them.

He got to the parking lot and his cell phone rang.

"Sergeant Cain."

"Bob?"

"Yes."

"Frank Cahalin here. How's it going?"

"Oh, hello, sir," Cain said. "It's going okay, I guess."

"You guys getting anywhere?"

Cain sighed. "I don't know."

"That doesn't sound too positive."

Cain said, "It is what it is."

"Did you get any more evidence against the drug dealer?"

"No. Not yet. But we're . . . no, we haven't got anything."

"Well, you need anything, you let me know."

"Yes, sir."

"You got plans for dinner?"

"Uh, well, the lieutenant wants me to interview a witness."

"Really? Who?"

"Some woman. It's nothing."

"Why do you say that?"

"Well, it's some woman that one of the deputies knew years ago. We're grasping for straws."

"What's the woman's name?" Frank said, "I can run it through our database."

Cain looked at the paper Hastings gave him. "Sharon Dunphy," he said. "Apparently, Hummel helped her out years ago. She's not a suspect, though."

After a moment, Frank said, "Hmmm."

"Yeah, well. He says I got to check it out."

"Yeah. Well, you got to do what — you got to do," Frank said. "You going to interview her now?"

"Yeah," Cain said. "Maybe we can have dinner another time, though. Thanks for calling."

A moment passed before Frank spoke.

"Sure," he said.

THIRTY-FOUR

Jimmy Rizza had learned automobile repair from the Illinois Department of Corrections. They had taught him the workings of engines and transmissions. In prison he learned that MacPherson struts were not designed by Porsche, but by a Ford engineer. He developed a fondness for the large, two-door, pillarless coupes made in the sixties and early seventies. When he was tipped off in Chicago years earlier, he had to leave behind his 1964 Ford Galaxie. He had spent seventeen months cherrying it out. The Galaxie, like most American cars of its time, had not been built for fast highway travel. The design of its undercarriage would not allow it to cruise steadily beyond eighty mph. It could be modified, though. Many cars like it had raced on NASCAR tracks alongside similar behemoths from Chrysler and General Motors. It could be modified for speed if you knew how to do it. He still missed that car.

He liked the feel of a garage. The smell, the comfort of machines and parts, the sound of an engine finding its pitch, styles of a past era. He and Dillon had done a lot of business out of a garage in Chicago. He helped Dillon direct narcotics traffic and payoffs, wearing grease-stained coveralls while he did it.

Now, he had an Oldsmobile Cutlass on the lift, replacing the brakes. Dillon would be here soon and he would change out of the coveralls and they would go and get the woman.

"Hello, Jimmy."

Jimmy turned around. Jack. Holding a pistol by his side.

For a few seconds neither one of them said anything. Jimmy held on to his socket wrench.

Jimmy said, "I see you're still using a .45."

"Yeah."

"I told you before, they're too loud. With a .22, no one hears unless they're close."

"Yeah," Regan said. "But then you have to get close yourself."

"How did you get in?"

"Through the bathroom window."

Jimmy held the socket wrench at his side. Regan said, "You got anything in your pockets, Jimmy?"

"No."

"Well, keep your hands out of them just the same."

Jimmy said, "You killed Sean."

"Yes I did," Regan said. He shook his head. "That was your fault, Jimmy. You shouldn't've brought him into it."

"You came after me first."

"I'm not after you. I'm after Mike. It's Mike Zans wants, not you."

"What did Mike do to Zans?"

Regan frowned. "Jimmy, come on. It's me here."

"Mike's got no beef with Zans."

"I *know*, Jimmy."

"What?"

"He ratted on him, Jimmy. You both did."

"Who told you that?"

"They told me about Mike. They didn't say anything about you. I figured that out myself."

"Me?"

"Yeah, you."

"You calling me a fucking rat?"

"Jimmy, I don't care. I'm just telling you I know. Zans doesn't know, but I do. I didn't come for you."

"The hell you say."

"I only looked for you because I knew

you'd know where Mike is. You take me to him and we're done."

"Jack, I don't know where he is."

"Jimmy," Regan said, and sighed. "How long we known each other? You think I don't know when you're lying?"

"I don't."

Regan raised the .45. "I'm going to count to three."

"Hey —"

"One."

"— hey —"

"Two."

"Hey . . . hey. All right, all right." Jimmy said, "Let's talk for a minute."

"Go ahead."

Jimmy said, "I tell you where he is, you gonna clip him?"

"Yeah."

"Guarantee that?"

"What do you mean guarantee?"

"What I mean is, if you don't, if you shoot and you miss, we're both dead. You point a gun at Mike, you better kill him."

"He's not indestructible, Jimmy."

"Yeah, well, the jury's out on that one."

"You've been hanging around him too long," Regan said. "He's got you believing his blarney."

"We're talking about Mike Dillon here."

"His time has come. Everybody's time comes sooner or later."

"Like Sean's?"

"Ah, Jimmy. You can't be mad at me for that. Would you have me lie down and let him kill me, let him kill my wife?"

"Yeah, I would. The way you were acting, I had good reason to think you were trying to clip me. Why didn't you just tell Max or Sean that it was Mike you were after?"

"Because they wouldn't have known," Regan said. He was feeling tired now. He said, "What difference does it make now? You're alive and if you take me to Mike, you get to stay alive. You protect Mike, you die. Now we both know if it were the other way around, Mike wouldn't hesitate for a second to give you up."

Jimmy Rizza said nothing.

Regan said, "If you haven't figured that out by now, you're not as smart as I thought you were."

Jimmy said, "What you're saying is, I don't give you an answer you like, you're going to clip me."

"Yeah, that's about the size of it."

"Okay, then. Yeah, he's in Saint Louis. I know where he lives and I can take you there now, if you like. But it won't be necessary. He's on his way here now."

Regan cocked his head. "Why's that?" he said.

Jimmy shrugged. "He wants me to help him take care of a woman."

"What, you mean kill her?"

"Yeah."

"What for?"

Jimmy shrugged. "She wants to break up with him."

Regan shook his head. "Fucking animal," he said. "Okay, we wait then." Regan gestured with the gun to some chairs near the workbench.

THIRTY-FIVE

Late evening. The sun had set against the November gray. The air was cold and dry. Murph drove the unmarked Impala south on Grand Avenue. Turned west on the second street past Tower Grove Park and then they were on a narrow street lined with houses and cars. After the next stop sign, Cain said, "That's it."

It was a dark redbrick house, divided into two homes. Two numbers, two mailboxes. There were separate steps leading up to the same porch area, divided by a low brick wall.

Murph slowed the car.

Cain said, "Where do people park here?" It was not a bad neighborhood, better than it had been ten years ago. But Cain spoke of it like it was a dump.

"They have spaces off the alley," Murph said. "Or you park on the street. There's a place up there."

They parked the car near the end of the block and walked back to the house.

They rang the doorbell twice before Sharon Dunphy answered it.

Cain showed her his police identification.

"Ms. Dunphy?"

"Yes?"

"I'm Sergeant Detective Cain. This is Detective Murphy. St. Louis PD. We'd like to ask you a few questions."

The woman looked them over. She stayed at the door.

"What about?"

"It's about something that involved you and your neighbor three years ago. May we come in?"

"I have to pick up my children soon," she said.

Cain said, "It won't take long."

"Well . . . okay."

She led them into the house. There was no foyer. Once they walked through the front door, they were in the living room, where they could see a green sofa that looked like it had been handed down and a recliner and an armchair. Sharon Dunphy picked up a remote control off the coffee table and switched off the television. The three of them looked at the blank television screen for a moment and then she said,

"What is it?" She was still standing.

The detectives stopped. Like a man leaning in for a kiss and getting a firm hand push on the chest. *That's as far as you go, buster.* Apparently, they were to question her on their feet, in front of the blank television screen.

Cain said, "About three years ago, you were having trouble with a neighbor who was bullying you, hassling your family. A police officer named Chris Hummel helped you out."

Sharon said, "Chris who?"

Cain said, "Chris Hummel. He was a deputy with the sheriff's office. You remember it, don't you?"

The woman looked off to the side, like she was thinking about it. She said, "No, I can't say I remember that. I never reported anything to the police."

Sergeant Cain and Detective Murphy looked at each other. They had seen this sort of side look many times before. Any police officer has. It's not even necessary to have received formal training in interrogation. In traffic, it's the look the bleary-eyed driver gives when asked how much he's had to drink. The look that reveals that the person has made a conscious decision not to tell the truth, but needs a moment to come up with a lie that he thinks is credible. They search for that lie offstage.

Murph said, "We know you didn't report it, ma'am. But Deputy Hummel did help you out, didn't he?"

"I really don't remember."

Cain said, "You remember Trudy West, don't you?"

"Uh, yes."

"We've already spoken with her. She told us about it."

"Told you about what?"

The detectives were silent.

And Sharon said, "I mean, I haven't seen Trudy in over two years."

Murph said, "Trudy West told us that you had trouble with a neighbor three years ago. That she put you in touch with Chris Hummel, and Chris Hummel had some words with this neighbor of yours and then the trouble stopped. Now, we want to know more about that."

"About what happened over three years ago?"

"Yes," Murph said.

Cain said, "Ms. Dunphy, you seem awfully nervous. Is there something you want to tell us?"

Sharon Dunphy had a husband in prison, had known men who had been criminals.

But she was at root a decent woman. She was not a practiced liar. And this was apparent now to the two detectives.

"No," she said. "Seriously, I have to pick up my children."

Murph said, "Do you know why we're here?"

"I —"

"You know Deputy Hummel was killed a few nights ago. You know about that, don't you?"

"I . . . Yes, I saw it on television."

Cain said, "What do you know about it?"

"I don't know anything."

"Ma'am." It was Murph speaking now. His voice firm, yet almost kind and solicitous. "You seem like you're about to cry. Is there something you want to tell us?"

"No. Look, Chris helped me out years ago. That's all I can tell you."

Murph said, "When's the last time you saw Chris?"

"What?"

"When — is — the — last time — you saw Chris?"

"I don't know."

Cain said, "Was it in the last two weeks?"

"— it —"

"It was, wasn't it?" Cain said. "You saw him in the last two weeks." He was aware now that they had stumbled on something.

She could not even look at them anymore. Tears forming now.

Murph said, "Are you scared?"

She gave out an involuntary sob. "I have to . . . my children . . ."

"Tell us," Murph said. "We're here to help you. Are you scared for your children?"

She tried to stop crying. Tried, but she couldn't stem it. She hadn't been ready for it. Hadn't been ready for two detectives to just march up to her front door and start asking questions about Chris Hummel. If she had known they were coming, she could have prepared for it. She could have done *something.*

Murph said, "Where are your children now?"

"One is at basketball practice. The other is at a friend's house. I have to get them. . . . I have to . . ."

"We can go with you," Murph said. "We can pick them up together. We won't let anyone hurt them. Do you understand that? We won't allow it. But you know something about this and you have to help us."

"I can't help you," she said.

"I promise you," Murph said, "I swear to you, we will protect your children. You have to let us help you."

293

"I don't know anything."

Cain said, "You saw Chris recently, before he was murdered, didn't you?"

She didn't answer. Looked away.

Cain said, "Did he hurt you?"

A moment before the woman shook her head.

Cain said, "Was he trying to help you?"

No response.

"He was, wasn't he?" Cain said. "He was trying to help you and it got him in trouble, didn't it."

She was crying. Crying and she couldn't stop.

"Didn't it?" Cain said.

"Jesus Christ," Murph said to himself, not believing it, but it was there in front of them now and they had it in their hands. He looked over at Cain. He said, "We're going to have to take her downtown."

"Right," Cain said. He had discovered the biggest break of the most important homicide case in years. Yet he felt no exhilaration. Only a sadness. He looked back at Murphy. "The children," he said.

Murph said, "We'll call dispatch from the car. Have units pick them up." He looked at Sharon Dunphy. "They'll be safe now."

Minutes later, they were out on the front

porch. The Dunphy woman in her coat, locking the door behind her. The detectives in front. They heard the lock click into place. And when they turned, there was a man on the pathway leading up to the steps, between the porch and street. The man was middle-aged, wearing a black jogging outfit. About thirty feet away. The detectives heard the Dunphy woman gasp.

The man stopped and turned around to walk away.

"Hey," Cain said. "Stop." He moved down the steps. "Hey, come here," he said.

And then it was happening.

The man turned back and Murph saw the glint of steel in the darkness. Cain reached inside his jacket but it was too late. Dillon shot Bobby Cain twice.

Murph saw the sergeant go down. He grabbed the woman and pushed her down behind the low brick wall with his right hand, then used that same hand to reach into his jacket for his service weapon. Dillon shot twice more and the second shot caught Murph in the upper thigh, and Murph shot back once, twice, three times, shot out in the dark, shooting at Dillon, who stood shooting at him before he gave it up and started running away and Murph collapsed on the porch, looked to his left to see the shadow fleeing in the night. Murph shot another round at the shadow, and then the shadow was gone.

THIRTY-SIX

There was the sound of the burbling engine, its pitch increasing as it accelerated away from the stop sign, decreasing as the Jaguar slowed to a stop, its headlights beaming on patrol cars and ambulances.

Hastings and Rhodes got out of the Jaguar.

They ran up to the front of the house and a group of patrol officers and a paramedic standing around a body, a second paramedic crouching. One of the officers held his cap in front of him.

A young patrolman turned and recognized them.

"He's dead, Lieutenant. He took two shots, one pierced his heart."

Hastings exhaled.

"Where's the other detective?"

"He's in the ambulance. He took a shot in the thigh. It went out the back."

None of the patrol officers or the paramedics offered the consolation that it was only a "flesh wound." They all knew that a bullet that goes through the front tumbles out the back with a mass of blood and flesh and muscle the size of a fist. If you're lucky, it misses the bone.

The young patrolman said, "We've got the woman in the unit over there. In case you want to talk to her."

Hastings nodded.

Bobby Cain lay on his back with his face to the heavens. His mouth and eyes were open. His overcoat was open and the sides lay on the ground like a beach towel.

"Howard," Hastings said, "take the woman out of the patrol unit and put her in my car." Hastings handed Rhodes his car keys. "Take her back to the station. Keep her there. Don't let anyone talk to her. No one. Is that clear?"

"Yes, sir."

"I'm going to the hospital with Murph. I'll be there as soon as I can."

Rhodes walked off to the patrol car.

Hastings moved closer to the body.

Forty minutes ago, the man had been in front of his desk, giving him shit. Talking, arguing, being Bobby Cain. Living. Angry because he believed Hastings was giving him a chickenshit assignment, trying to put him in his place. It wasn't a personal thing, but Cain acted like it was. He had not understood that all of the tasks could seem meaningless and pointless until they weren't. Hastings had to assign men to certain jobs and if egos got bruised, that was tough. And now there was this.

Hastings lowered himself to one knee, got closer to the man.

"Oh, Jesus," Hastings said. "Cain."

Cain. What was it about Cain? What was it that had always bothered him? Had Cain betrayed him in some way? Had Cain not respected him enough? Hastings feared that it was neither of those things. He knew the answer and it shamed him. In fact, he knew the answer had little to do with the fact that Cain was pretty much impossible to like. The truth was, Cain would frustrate him by surprising him. Hastings had wanted Cain to be dumb, but he was smart. He had wanted Cain to be lazy, but he was diligent. Had wanted him to be a bad detective, but the man had had good instincts for the work. Try as he might, Hastings could not deny that.

Why? Why had Cain done this? He could have been a lawyer. He could have used his father's influence to coast through life. He could have passed this by. Why did he *choose* to do it? What possessed the stupid son of a bitch to go into law enforcement? Why couldn't he have just remained a punk?

Hastings choked it back. Then he reached out and placed a hand on Robert Cain's shoulder.

"Rest in peace, brother."

Murph lay on a stretcher in the ambulance. The back doors shut and the ambulance began to move. Hastings sat next to the paramedic who was attending to the victim of the gunshot. They had Murph on an IV, finger probes measuring oxygen and saturation.

"Murph," Hastings said. "We'll be at Barnes soon. You're going to be all right." He said, "Can you to talk to me?"

Murph squeezed his eyes shut then open. He was going into shock.

Murph said, "Cain . . ."

"He's dead."

". . . thought . . . so . . ." He closed his eyes again.

Hastings said, "Murph, I need to know what happened. Please."

"We got . . . there . . . right . . . away, we . . . knew . . . knew she knew . . . something . . ."

"She knows Hummel?"

Murph nodded.

". . . She's seen him . . . lately. . . . She was . . . trying . . . to lie to us . . . couldn't lie . . ."

"What did you get out of her?"

". . . Not much. . . . We were going to . . . bring her in . . . got outside . . . the guy, coming up the walk . . ."

"The guy that shot Cain?"

". . . Yeah. . . . Middle-aged, average height . . . black track suit . . . tried to walk away. Cain . . . Cain said 'stop' . . . turned around and . . . shot . . . shot Cain . . . me . . ."

"You return fire?"

Murph nodded. "I didn't . . . hit him, I think . . ."

Hastings set his fingers lightly on the detective's forearm.

"Cain," Murph said.

"Yeah, I know," Hastings said.

". . . Kids . . ."

"Yes?"

"The woman . . . she's worried . . . about her kids . . . scared, I believe . . ."

The siren wailed through red lights at intersections, slipped through parting traffic.

Hastings said, "I'll have someone call your wife." Hastings would have preferred to do it himself, but there wasn't time.

301

THIRTY-SEVEN

A black and red Laclede cab came to a stop in front of downtown headquarters. Hastings paid the driver and ran into the building. When he got upstairs he found Karen Brady waiting for him. Standing in the hall with her hands in her pockets.

She said, "What happened?"

"Cain is dead. Shot."

"I know that," she said. "What happened?"

"They went to interview a witness. Sharon Dunphy. A woman Chris Hummel knew. She knows something of this. They were leaving and they got ambushed."

Karen Brady, red-faced and scared, would not be able to tell the brass to refer their questions to Hastings. They would expect to hear it from her first. She said, "Did you send Cain there?"

"Yes," he said. "I sent Cain and Murphy there." It seemed necessary to point that out.

She stared at him.

And Hastings said, "Captain, I have to go."

"Go? You got a date?"

"Sharon Dunphy's here. I need to question her immediately. She's the key to this. It's our first real break."

"Is that what you call this?"

"I'm sorry, Karen. I have to talk to her right now. Please."

"Maybe we should wait."

Hastings took a breath, exhaled. "Why?" he said.

"The assistant chief will be here soon. He wants to talk to you."

"Then let me know when he gets here," Hastings said. "Excuse me." He walked away before she could say anything else. Hopefully, she would think he had misunderstood her. If she didn't, fuck her.

Down the hall, he went through a door and shut it behind him. An interrogation room. Rhodes stood on this side of a two-way mirror. On the other side of the mirror was Sharon Dunphy. Wearing her coat like a blanket. Her face was tear-stained.

Hastings said, "We get her children?"

"Yes," Rhodes said. "They're downstairs with a uniform."

"Who?"

"Bennett."

303

"Okay."

"What's the word on Murph?"

"He's in ICU. Lost a lot of blood, but he's stable."

Rhodes said, "George, I —"

"How is she?" Hastings said. He knew Rhodes was going to say something about Cain, but he didn't have time for it right now.

Rhodes stopped. For perhaps the first time, he wondered if he liked the lieutenant.

Rhodes said, "Scared."

"Okay." Hastings turned toward Rhodes. "Is the videotape running?"

"Yes."

"Turn it off, will you?"

The quiet request made Rhodes wonder again. "Yes, sir," he said. He switched off the recorder.

Hastings said, "I'd like you to stay out here, if you don't mind."

"Okay."

Hastings walked into the interview room and shut the door behind him. The Dunphy woman looked up at him. Hastings remained standing.

"I'm Lieutenant Hastings. Homicide. Who was the man on your sidewalk tonight?"

The woman shook her head. "It was

dark," she said.

Hastings said, "Do you want your children to die?"

Behind the observation window, Detective Rhodes winced.

The woman said, "No."

"Is that what you're afraid of? Or is that just some line of shit you give policemen before you get them killed?"

The woman's face twisted as she tried to hold back tears. "What are you talking about?"

"Answer that question."

"I . . . didn't want to hurt anybody."

"Whether you meant to or not doesn't make much difference. Not to Detective Cain or the other two officers."

"You think I planned that?"

"I don't know."

"You . . . you've no —"

"No what?"

". . . No right . . ."

"Lady, I've got three dead police officers and at least two of them are connected to you. Don't speak to me of what's right. Let me lay it out for you: I am this close to charging you with conspiracy to commit murder. You'll be placed in county until trial and I will ensure that any bail will be denied. Who will protect your children then?"

"You can't . . . you can't do that."

"Lady, it's done unless you tell me that man's name right now."

"Where are my children now?"

Hastings said, "I don't know."

"You don't — but they promised me they'd pick them up. *They promised.*"

"I'm the dealmaker now. Give me that man's name and I'll have them picked up immediately. Otherwise, I'll see you in the morning."

"You can't do that." She was on the point of wailing now. "What are you?"

"The name," Hastings said. "Now. Or I walk out the door." He started walking.

When he was at the door, she said, "Mike."

He stopped.

"Mike who?"

"Mike Dillon. He's from Chicago."

Hastings read reports, national dispatches in his spare time. He looked at the window, knowing that Rhodes was watching him. Maybe wanting to strangle him by now. Hastings said, "You mean Mike Dillon the mobster?"

The woman slowly nodded.

Hastings looked at the window again. He

lifted his arm and made a flicking switch with his index finger. On the other side, Rhodes flipped the recording device on.

Hastings said, "Did he kill Hummel?"

"Yes."

"Why?"

"Chris ran into me . . . at a convenience store. He's . . . he was an old friend. He could see that something was wrong. But I wouldn't tell him. So he came by my house that night to talk to me. I didn't tell him about Mike. About Mike being in my life. Mike must have seen him there. I swear, I swear on my children I did not set him up. I swear on my children. I had no idea Mike was going to do that. I saw it on television, like everyone else."

"Why didn't you come forward? After it was done, why didn't you come forward?"

"What would you have done? Police, mob, it's all the same. You just threatened to let my children die."

Hastings sighed.

"Your children are downstairs," he said. "They've been here the whole time."

She stared at him for a moment, a look of complete revulsion.

"You bastard," she said.

Hastings said, "Cain had children too, lady." He motioned for Rhodes to come in.

Hastings said, "Detective Rhodes is going to bring your children in here so you'll know I'm telling you the truth. You get ten minutes with them. Then you and I talk some more."

"I have rights," she said.

"No one's arresting you," Hastings said. "Now, tell us where this man lives."

THIRTY-EIGHT

They packed into the station briefing room. Hastings stood at the front of the room, still in plainclothes, Karen on one side of him, Rhodes on the other. Hastings had insisted Rhodes stand up there with him. Beyond them was a sea of cops, most of them dressed in the green military-looking jumpsuits with black turtleneck sweaters underneath. In black stencil on their backs, it read POLICE TACTICAL UNIT. There were about thirty of them. Another twenty cops, some in uniform, some in plainclothes. Facing them was Charlie Day, captain of the tact team, Ronnie Wulf, chief of detectives, Chief Mark Grassino, and Assistant Chief Fenton Murray. Aaron Pressler, the department's media spokesman, leaned against the door with his back, as if to keep civilians from interrupting. The St. Louis county sheriff and his chief deputy were there also. Everyone aware of the others in the room, of the task before them. Scared, but excited and hungry too, wanting to bring this fiend down. In their more honest moments, they would admit personal dislikes for at least someone else in the briefing room. At other times, the normal human emotions of envy, resentment, pettiness, and anger would surface among them. But on this night, they all took comfort in the fraternity, the brotherhood. On this night, they shared the same determination.

Chief Grassino stood in front of the podium.

"The target's name is Michael Dillon," Grassino said. "We have his summary sheet, but most of you are not going to have time to read that. He is the chief suspect in the murders of Deputies Chris Hummel and Wade Childers and Sergeant Robert Cain. This man is a professional killer. He is smart and he is tough. We believe that for that past year and a half he has been living in St. Louis under the name of Jerry Rosinski."

Behind Chief Grassino on a white screen there was a grainy black and white photograph of Mike Dillon, set against a gray wall of a building. He wore sunglasses and a light-colored windbreaker.

Grassino said, "Our information is that he is residing in a small two-story house on

4351 Reno Street. Near the Hill. Captain Day of the tact team has obtained the floor plans of the house and he will brief the members of the tact team on those. Presently we have patrol units guarding the back and the front, waiting for us. Lieutenant Hastings has obtained both a search warrant and an arrest warrant. As this is a high-risk search, it is my order that the detectives remain on the outer perimeter until the raid is concluded. Once Dillon is secured or it is determined absolutely that he is not there, the homicide detectives and technicians will be allowed in."

Grassino turned and briefly regarded Hastings. Hastings nodded an affirmation back. It wasn't necessary, Hastings thought. Established procedure prohibited detectives from being primary in high-risk situations akin to combat, but Hastings was grateful to Grassino nonetheless for taking the step of letting the officers know he was not a coward. A small gesture, but a mark of a natural leader.

Grassino turned back to the officers. "I guess that's about it. You've all been well trained, and you don't need me to tell you how to do your jobs. Good luck."

Twenty-five minutes later, Hastings and

Rhodes sat in the Jaguar, parked three blocks down the street from the house on Reno Street. Parked one block beyond the outer perimeter. The second level of security was the inner perimeter, consisting entirely of tact team members surrounding the house. The last and most dangerous level was the entry team, the officers who would be going in; tact team officers were stacked up on the front and rear security at the back door.

In the Jaguar, Rhodes released the safety on his service weapon, a .357 semiautomatic. Hastings's gun, a .38 Chiefs Special snubnose revolver, did not have a safety.

Rhodes said, "It's cold."

"Yeah," Hastings said.

"Do you think he's there?"

"I don't know."

"Man," Rhodes said. It had only been a few hours. Cain was dead and it hadn't sunk in. A shooting that led to a witness and then an identifiable suspect and an address. Another police officer dead, sacrificed, perhaps to find the killer of the first two.

"George?"

"Yes."

"It just happened, you know. Who would know?"

"Right. Who would know."

Hastings was feeling it. His body temperature up and his palms sweaty. They were at a safe distance, but there were men and a few women going into the house of a man who used machine guns on police officers. He wanted the time to pass. He wanted it to be done. He wanted Dillon shot in the head before he knew it was happening.

"We'll get him," Rhodes said.

And Hastings was thinking, yeah, maybe. If the guy was your typical dumbass criminal shooter, he wouldn't think to hide. He'd be in the house registered in his alias watching cable television with three or four beers in him. Look up in shock as twenty to thirty cops in black Kevlar stormed in his house and made him piss down both legs. Put his face down into the sofa as he cries out for help, the loser within hoping for capture in some way. More often than not, that's how it went. But a handful of them were smart. They cleared out before the police got there. They thought things through and made contingency plans. Mike Dillon's file suggested he wasn't a typical dumbass. If he wasn't in the house, he would probably leave town. He would probably have money stashed someplace and a clean car and he would take one of two dozen roads out of town. He would be gone in the night. Dillon had time. He had shot Cain and the ambulances had come and the woman was questioned and the warrants were obtained and there was a pre-arrest briefing. All of it necessary, all of it eating time.

Rhodes peered through the windshield.

"There they go," he said.

A muffled blast and flash in the distance. Stun grenades. Curt commands barked out.

Rhodes said, "I think they're in the house now."

Ram smashing in the deadbolt on the front door. On the back door, they used the shotgun with a shell designed to blow the hinges off the doors. Officers running in, more commands, breaking off in twos, every closed door and unexamined corner a threat.

Three minutes went by. Then another two.

The handheld radio squawked. Hastings picked it up.

"Yeah."

"Captain Day here."

"Yeah."

"He's not here."

The man was a captain and he knew his business and he deserved respect. But Hastings couldn't help asking.

"You sure?"

"He's not here," Day said. "You can bring your men in now."

THIRTY-NINE

"Jimmy, you're lying to me."

Rizza said, "I swear, on my mother, he called before you got here. He said he was coming."

"Here?"

"Yeah, here. Jack, I know where he lives. You want, we can get in the car and drive over to his house. But I'm telling you, if we do, he's probably going to get here after we do."

"It's been well over an hour."

Rizza shrugged. "What do you want me to do?"

"Call him."

"Okay, but he's not going to be there."

"Call him."

Regan kept the gun on Jimmy as he walked over to the telephone hanging on the wall.

Hastings was not in the kitchen when it went off. The detectives and technicians all knew better than to touch the phone with bare hands. The suspect's phone was under no circumstances to be used to place calls. But it was ringing now so a detective ran to the front of the house and called for Hastings, the supervising detective.

Hastings rushed back, looked at the phone. There was no answering machine and they had not been there long enough to set up a listening device to it. It rang twice more before he picked it up, his hand in a latex glove.

Hastings said, "Yeah?"

"Mike?"

Hastings grunted. "Yeah?"

"It's Jimmy. Where the hell are you?"

Hastings said, "Where are you?"

"I'm at the garage."

There was a silence.

Shit.

Jimmy Rizza said, "Who is this?"

Hastings bit his lower lip. He said, "Who is *this*?"

Jimmy hung up the phone.

Regan said, "Well?"

Jimmy said, "That wasn't him."

Regan sighed. "Jimmy."

"It wasn't. Fuck, I don't know who it was."

Regan raised the pistol.

"Jack, *fuck,* I don't. I don't fucking know."

"Jimmy —"

"Christ, I'm telling you, that was not Mike. I don't know who the fuck it was."

"Jimmy."

"Jack, the whole time, we've been in this town, I have never heard anyone else answer that goddamn phone but Mike. For all's I know, it's someone working for you."

Regan hesitated.

"It's no one I know," Regan said. "I came alone. I always do." He pointed the barrel of the gun at Jimmy's kneecap.

"*Jack.* I swear —"

The telephone rang.

Regan's eye was on the end of the gun, the sight resting on the knee. It would cripple Jimmy and start him screaming and he would stop fucking around like a little kid. Shatter the kneecap and not bleed out and then he could get some answers.

The telephone rang.

"Jack, that might be him. Let me answer it."

The telephone rang.

Jimmy started backing away to the phone, his hands raised, fingertips quivering.

"Okay?" Jimmy said. "Just let me see."

The telephone rang and Jimmy picked it up.

"Hello," Jimmy said.

"It's me," Dillon said. "We got problems."

Jimmy said, "What's going on?"

"I don't know," Dillon said. "You tell me."

Jimmy said, "What are you talking about?"

"You got cops there?"

"What?"

"You heard me. Are the police there?"

It came back to Jimmy now. *Who is this?* A man's voice he hadn't heard before. A policeman. Immediately, he decided not to tell Mike.

"No," Jimmy said. "Man, what's up with you?"

Dillon said, "I got about a hundred of them surrounding my house now. Looks like they called in the fucking marines."

"Jesus."

"Yeah. You know anything about it?"

"Mike, I didn't say a fucking word."

Dillon was calling from a pay phone at a gas station. His Cadillac was parked on the side. He kept his back turned against the night traffic, but occasionally turned his head back to look for patrol vehicles.

He said, "Yeah, well, there was some trouble at Sharon's place."

"Sharon's place? Hey, I thought you were going to come here first."

"Change of plans," Dillon said. "We gotta

319

leave town, Jimmy."

"Mike, did you take care of her yourself?"

"No," Dillon said. "She's alive. That's the problem. We have to go."

A policeman answering Dillon's home phone. *Who is this?* Jimmy said, "Mike, what did you do?"

"I clipped a couple of cops. And if I go down, you're going down too. Understand?"

Jimmy Rizza looked at Jack Regan's .45 and remembered the cop's voice on the phone. Man, when it rains it pours. Jimmy said, "Yeah, I understand."

"Good," Dillon said. "The way I figure it, we both need to get out of here."

"Okay, Mike. Whatever you say. Why don't you come out here?"

"No way," Dillon said. "You come and meet me. Bring the Thunderbird, you understand? You have to bring the Thunderbird. You show up in something else, I'm liable to be disappointed."

"All right, Mike. Where?"

"The Savvis Center. Mezzanine, section 307. Remember, bring the Thunderbird."

Dillon hung up the phone.

Jimmy put his receiver back on the wall. He said, "He wants me to meet him."

Regan said, "Where?"

"The Savvis Center. You know, where the

320

hockey team plays."

"You should have told him to come here."

"Jack, the police are surrounding his house. He's afraid they might be here too. It doesn't matter what I say or what you do, he's not going to come here."

A big sports arena, Regan thought. He wants the protection of a crowd.

Jimmy pointed to a 1989 beige Ford Thunderbird. "We're supposed to come in that," he said.

Regan glanced at the car. He pictured a gun hidden under the front seat, or in a secret panel on the driver's side door. He almost smiled.

"No," Regan said.

"He *insisted,* Jack. You know how he is."

Regan said, "It's not going to matter, though. Is it?"

Jimmy sighed. "No, I guess it won't."

The telephone started ringing again.

Jimmy looked at the phone for a moment. Christ. Raining. He said to Regan, "I'm ready."

It was still ringing when they left.

Contrary to film lore, modern-day technology can trace a telephone call the instant the call is placed. A civilian with *69 capacity knows that much. Soon they had the address of Rizza's garage, which they would later learn was registered to another alias of his, and they sent a couple of radio cars immediately.

In the rear foyer at the house registered to Jerry Rosinski, they found a dog crate with a terrier mix inside. The dog was frightened and curled in the corner. A uniformed officer took his head gear off and showed the little dog a human face and coaxed it out. The detectives suggested that they take the dog out to the front yard so it wouldn't mess up evidence or shit in the house.

Rhodes said, "Maybe he'll come back for the dog."

Hastings said, "I doubt it. *Fuck.* Let me think here." He said, "The guy on the phone said, where are you?"

"Yeah?"

"So he was expecting him."

"Yeah, maybe."

"Like, what's holding you up, where are you."

Rhodes said, "You want to go out there?"

"Yeah," Hastings said. "Listen, you stay here. Call me if you find something. Something that will tell me that this guy's not halfway to Canada by now."

Forty

The St. Louis Blues were on the road. The event this night was indoor soccer; St. Louis Steamers playing the Baltimore Blast. It was seven bucks a ticket at the gate. When Dillon got there, they were still introducing the players. Wiry young guys running through steam in the dark, coming out under individual spotlights. *Shaun David! . . . Jes-Se Elmore! . . . Ibrahim Kante! . . .* The announcer let the crowd know if a player was from St. Louis.

It took Dillon back to a time when he watched a jai alai game in Miami. Some cluck told him he should invest in it because it was going to be as big as hockey. Bigger, maybe. Dillon had passed.

It was hokey, this indoor soccer. Guys kicking the ball against the wall so that it would bounce back to another player and maybe he could get a goal, or bounce it off someone's face and halt the whole stupid process for a couple of minutes. He couldn't believe people paid money to see it. He was vaguely aware they had an indoor soccer team in Chicago. In Baltimore too, apparently. St. Louis was not Chicago. It wasn't Baltimore either. But it was a *city*. And now he would have to leave. Go back on the road to small towns like El Dorado, Kansas, or Creston, Iowa, or any other number of towns where he had spent ten years leaving cash in safety deposit boxes. Go back to living like a fucking nomad. He hoped he could skip that route this time. With the money he had hidden in the Thunderbird he could go straight to Montreal, maybe live like a human being for a few years. Hang with people who spoke French and didn't give him the proper respect, but at least be able to get a decent cup of coffee.

Down to his left he saw Jimmy. Coming around the corner and looking up at him.

Jimmy stopped.

He stood about ten feet from the wall of the stairwell.

Jimmy motioned for him to come down.

What was this?

Dillon motioned for Rizza to come up to sit next to him. Jimmy shook his head, motioned for Mike to come down.

Dillon looked around. The lights on the

floor were on now, the players running around. He could see the spectators around him, make out the colors of their jackets and caps. No blue uniforms in sight. Dillon got out of his seat and started to walk down toward Jimmy.

He reached the front of the section on the other side and began walking toward Rizza.

Jimmy's hands were out of his pockets now, gesturing a shrug of sorts.

Dillon stopped. He motioned to Jimmy to come toward him.

And then Jimmy froze.

Dillon knew. He knew it as the deer knows the wolf's scent. He began backing away.

Jimmy said, "Mike!"

Regan stepped out, Jimmy Rizza partially between them now, and Dillon drew a pistol from his jacket pocket and fired.

Regan wasn't ready for it. The first shot took Jimmy in the chest, the second went between Jimmy's body and arm and went through Regan's side, and then Jimmy was thrown back against Regan and they were both on the ground, Dillon running away now.

Dillon got to the end of the section and ran down the stairs. He got to the crowds milling at the concession area and put the

pistol back in his pocket, screams now coming from the arena. Dillon kept moving.

FORTY-ONE

"Judge Foley?"

"Yes?"

"This is Lieutenant Hastings. Sorry to bother you."

"That's okay. What's up?" She said, "Did you get him?" Judge Claire Foley had authorized the previous warrants.

"No." The only good news he could give her is that no more police officers had been shot. But it wasn't worth giving right now. He said, "He's not there. Listen, while we were there, he got a telephone call. From someone in a building near Arsenal Street."

"Okay."

"I tried to pass myself as Michael Dillon. It didn't work. The caller hung up. But the caller said, 'Where are you?' "

"So . . ."

"Where are you, like he was expecting him to be at that place. The place he was calling from."

"Oh."

"So —"

"So on the basis of that," Judge Foley said, "you think Dillon's at this address?"

Hastings was not at all sure, going on instinct and adrenaline as much as anything else. "Yes," he said firmly.

"I see. Are you en route now?"

"Yes, ma'am."

"Okay, Lieutenant. Give me the exact address and I'll authorize a telephonic warrant."

He managed to push Jimmy off of him. It wasn't easy; Jimmy was a big man, almost as big as Regan. Regan reached for the gun in his jacket. It was still there. Much good it had done him. Shit. He should have seen it coming. He should have known that Jimmy would tip Mike off. Either directly or indirectly; indirectly probably. A look of panic in the eyes, hands shaking, the way he stood . . . *something*, goddamn it. He had forgotten about Dillon. Dillon was smart and strong and he had a nose for these things. One of those rare humans who seemed to just sense traps. Dillon had not survived this long by being dumb. Dillon hunted was still Dillon. And Dillon was gone now and Jack Regan had a bullet in him.

Regan managed to get to his feet. He felt it then, bad. Unsteady, swaying but he stood still and concentrated on not falling down and kept on his feet. Man. He was aware of people around him, so many people, indistinct but close and more beyond; people screaming and shouting and questioning, people watching him, staring at the large wine-colored stain on the front of his jacket. The lights blurred around him. He told himself that he had to leave, had to move. There was a blanket in the car. What he had to do was get to the car and stuff the blanket into the gash in his side and stop the bleeding. Stop the bleeding and drive to Chicago and get to Sully. Sully the medicine man, Sully who had been a medic in one of the wars. . . . Sully would fix it and there would be no calls to the police reporting a gunshot wound. . . . Sully in Chicago . . . not too far from his place . . . in Chicago . . . Chicago . . . ? Chicago, bullshit. Who was here? Who was in this town 280 miles away from home? What support system, what . . . fucking . . . *network* did he have here? . . . Maybe he could call Zans and ask him if he knew a Sully in St. Louis. . . . Someone who would patch him up and send him on his . . . way

. . . Zans would know what to do. . . . Kate
. . . Kate would know, maybe . . . Zans . . .
shit, Zans was in jail . . . ?

People in the crowd pointed the man on
the ground out to a couple of security
guards near the concession stand. They
turned him over and took away his gun. One
of the guards felt Regan's neck.

The guard said, "This one's still
breathing."

Dillon walked out of the Savvis Center
among hundreds of murmuring, frightened
people. An announcer on the sound system
encouraged people not to panic or rush but
to quietly leave the arena.

He approached his car warily. He did not
want to believe that the police now had his
tag number and make of car, but believing
it was like hoping to fill an inside straight.
He thought about stealing another one, but
people kept pouring out of the arena and he
was afraid an owner would walk up as he
stole a car. And it had been several years
since he had stolen cars. He watched the
Cadillac for a minute or two and saw no
police around it. He walked to it, unlocked
it, and got in.

Had Jimmy brought the Thunderbird?
Had he done as he was told?

It was hard to know. The only thing he knew now is that Jimmy brought Jack Regan. Jack would not have wanted to accommodate Jimmy. Maybe they came in Jack's car. Maybe they didn't. If they came in the Thunderbird, it would not be possible to look for it around here. Not with police looking for him, maybe even looking for the Cadillac he was in. What was the joke from childhood? Why are you looking over here when you dropped it over there? Because the light's better over here. If Jimmy had left the Thunderbird at the garage, well, it would still be there. It would be easy to see, easy to get into and drive away.

Earlier, he had been worried that the cops were with Jimmy. Earlier, he had not known what to think. But Jimmy showed up with Jack, not a shitload of cops. So he had that much for going for him. So the cops had not been at the garage. Right. The cops had not been at the garage. If Jimmy had left the Thunderbird at the garage, it would still be there. If it were still there, he could dump the Caddy and drive away with the Thunderbird with eighty thousand dollars stuffed inside it.

It was worth a look.

Hastings pulled up to the garage. There were two patrol cars out front. Four officers, one of them approaching him as he got out of the Jaguar.

Sergeant Stanley Millburn. Hastings knew him.

"George."

"Hi, Stan. What do you know?"

Sergeant Millburn said, "We got here about ten minutes ago. We looked through the windows, didn't see anything. No one's here. No one we can see anyway."

Hastings said, "You didn't see anyone leave?"

"No." The sergeant said, "When did you get the call?"

"About fifteen minutes ago." Hastings sighed. "Shit."

Sergeant Millburn said, "What do you want to do, George?"

Hastings said, "I've got a telephonic search warrant from Judge Foley on my way over here. You guys got a ram?"

Sergeant Millburn called out. "Anyone got a ram?"

A patrol officer said he had one, and Sergeant Millburn told him to go ahead and get it.

When that was done, the five of them moved up to the door. Two officers in front, positioning the ram; two officers behind, one holding a shotgun, the other holding a Glock .40, the slide racked and ready. Hastings drew his .38 snub and held it at his side.

The standard procedure was to knock and call out, "Search warrant, search warrant," and on the third one smash in the door. But they weren't going to go through that shit tonight and give the animal on the other side any warning, real or imagined.

Millburn turned to Hastings and said, "Okay?"

Hastings looked up the street then down, hesitating . . .

His cell phone rang.

It made all of them jump in that quiet moment and then they felt silly and angry at the same time. "Christ," Hastings said and he was not the only one. Feeling dumb for not turning it off. Rookie mistake.

Hastings held up a hand, pausing the men, and then answered his phone.

"Hastings."

"Lieutenant? This is Sergeant Acey Rand. There's just been a shooting at the Savvis Center. The shooter's description matches your guy."

Hastings said, "Is he there?"

"No. We think he slipped out of the building in the crowd."

"What happened?"

"He shot two guys. They're not cops. One of them's dead, the other one's on his way to the hospital."

"Fuck," Hastings said. It was becoming a murder spree. A killer on the loose with nothing to lose. How many more corpses before the night was through? "All right," Hastings said. "Let me get back to you."

"Sure, Lieutenant."

Hastings switched off the phone, even though it seemed moot now. He stood immobile, staring ahead at nothing. The officers around him asked him no questions and looked at each other and made gestures.

Hastings turned to Sergeant Millburn.

Hastings said, "Change of plans."

Millburn said, "What?"

"That was Acey Rand. They think our man shot a couple of guys at the Savvis Center."

"They get him?"

"No," Hastings said. "Maybe he's on his way here."

"Why do you think that?"

"I don't know. It's a place he knows. He probably knows he can't go home. Maybe he'll come by here to use the toilet."

"Yeah, and maybe he's leaving town."

Hastings said, "If he is, he is. Nothing I can do about that now. But if he's coming here, we'll be ready for him. You got something better to do?"

"Well —"

"I don't. Let's wait here for an hour, see if he comes by."

The other officers were younger and unfamiliar with the detective. Two of them had never spoken with Hastings at all. They were in uniform and the lieutenant was in plainclothes. They would take their cue from the sergeant and the sergeant knew this. He knew Hastings too and thought well of his judgment, but a lot of years had passed.

The sergeant said, "All right, George. It's your call."

"Okay."

The sergeant said, "Shall we wait in there?"

"No. We ram the door, he'll be able to tell and then he'll drive right past. I want you to take your patrol car down two blocks that way, hide and wait. Another car down that way, same thing. I'll park over there."

It was probably a violation of two or three

policies and Hastings knew it. But if they called in more units and Dillon was coming, the presence of other units would run him off. There wasn't time to explain the wisdom of the plan to others and seek justification and authorization. Besides, he wasn't sure it was that wise to begin with.

FORTY-TWO

Hastings tucked the Jaguar around the corner in a parking lot with old pickups and classic autos that would never be restored. When he was done backing it in, the Jag faced the garage across the street. He shut the car off, got out, and walked out into the street.

An industrial area, bleak and dreary. Motor rebuilders, steel fabrication, heat exchangers, engine service, and auto parts. It thrummed with business in the decade following the Second World War, but had been in decay since the Johnson administration. Dark and cold now and no traffic in sight.

The patrol cars were hidden, two blocks west and three blocks east.

He walked back to the Jag and popped open the trunk. Took out an Ithaca pump shotgun, made sure it was loaded. He racked the slide and put one in the chamber. He got in the car and rested the shotgun on the passenger seat, his hand on the stock.

He waited.

He closed his eyes for a couple of seconds and thought of sitting behind a blind in Nebraska, sitting in cold and trying not to think about the freezing temperature, waiting for the sound of the deer rustling through the brush before it appeared.

The file on Dillon noted that he had gone underground the day before charges were filed against him in state court, Cook County. Chicago and state police had prepared the case against him. Racketeering, racketeering conspiracy, trafficking in narcotics. The guy had made millions extorting payments from bookies and drug dealers. No murder charges filed on him, but the paperwork showed that people around him tended to die or disappear.

Released from the federal penitentiary in 1982. No convictions since. No arrests.

No arrests?

How?

In many respects, George Hastings was a cautious man. He kept a lot of his opinions to himself. He was not politically ideological; it seemed like a lot of work to him. But he was aware enough to recognize that he was a moderately skilled diplomat himself. Not because he particularly wanted to be, but because he needed to be. It was a line you walked in police administration, maintaining self-respect while surviving the bear traps of departmental infighting and bureaucracy. When he was married, Eileen, a born snob, went to great lengths to establish friendships with people outside of law enforcement. Some of them were okay, some of them not; usually it didn't last. Hastings remembered having a tolerable conversation with a college professor at an otherwise dreadful dinner party. The guy had tenure at a state university and he complained about a bitter ongoing dispute. The guy said, "Do you know why the fighting is so intense? It's because the stakes are so low." And Hastings had smiled. The department could be like that. That was why it was best to keep your opinions to yourself. That was why he had revealed his mixed feelings about the death penalty only to Joe Klosterman, one of the few people he trusted fully. When Hastings thought about this in his quieter, more contemplative moments, he realized that his discomfort with state-sponsored execution stemmed, in some part, from his experience in dealing with a few judges and prosecutors stupid enough and arrogant enough to frighten him. But he also knew that he was uncomfortable with his own thoughts about it. Like the one he had now. The one that said, this man needs to die.

At an earlier time, the man needed to be put in a cage and kept there. It made no difference to Hastings if the cage was an isolated cell at Sing Sing or one with shag carpet and cable television. The man needed to be separated from civilized society. But someone had opened the man's cage and let him out. Let him roam and menace and kill. And now three police officers were dead. They could catch him now and put him back in his cage, but it wouldn't make Cain or Hummel or Deputy Childers any less dead.

Hastings heard something.

A car approaching.

Lights illuminated the street, pushed down the street and then it was there. A black Cadillac.

Hastings waited.

A man got out of the Caddy. It was him. He fit the description. It was the man from the photo, standing about forty yards away.

Hastings thought, get out of the car, put the shotgun on him, and order him to put his hands on the roof of the car. Do that . . .

Or call in the patrol cars?

No. He might be gone by then. Might hear the radio squawk. Might hear the cars approach and bolt. Might get away again . . .

Dillon looked around. Looked up and down the street. Did not see the detective across the street, hiding in his car in the shadows. He walked to the front door of the garage, unlocked it, and went in.

He flicked on the lights. For a moment, he actually expected to see Jimmy there. Weird. Honey, I'm home. Oh, yeah, he's not here. He got clipped.

The Thunderbird was here.

Good. Good call. Dillon wasn't sure if Jimmy knew about the eighty thousand hidden in the T-Bird. Maybe he had known and had taken it out. Maybe Jack had refused to let him take the car, thinking there would be a weapon hidden in there. Jack was smart that way. Smarter than Jimmy had been. But, Dillon thought, not smarter than me. He smiled at the sight of Jack falling back. Had he killed him? If there had been more time, fewer people, he would have walked over and made sure. Said something clever and final. *Hey, Jackie. How do you like St. Louis?* Then put a bullet in his head.

Then he saw it.

Light reflecting off the steel fabrication

building across the street. Sweeping then coming back onto the road.

It was enough.

Hastings called in the patrol cars on his handheld radio. He got out of the car and walked carefully across the street. Holding the shotgun with both hands, he approached the door. A block down, one of the patrol cars turned out into the street, headlights on, but no siren or flashers.

He heard it then, the machinery kicking on as the garage door began to open, to his right, and it was happening, the door halfway open as Hastings turned and the nose of the Thunderbird poked out and then the whole car as the engine roared and Hastings raised the shotgun and fired. Buckshot spattering the rear window of the car and then it was gone from that space and out into the street, in front of the patrol car and turning left, going around the two officers in their unit and Hastings couldn't fire another round for fear of hitting the officers.

Hastings yelled, "Get him." As if the men inside the car could hear and the patrol car reversed, tires squealing as they accelerated and flipped the car around, not quite 180 but almost, and the other patrol car whizzed by them to give chase.

Hastings ran across the street to the Jaguar.

Minutes later, he was trailing the two patrol cars, racing through intersections. In the distance, he could see the beige Thunderbird, its taillights bobbing up and down as it hit dips in the road going about eighty. God, Hastings thought. It could get bad. A killer with absolutely nothing to lose, blowing through a red light and slamming into a van with a family inside. It could get very bad.

The Thunderbird slowed, without hitting the brakes, and then made a left at the next intersection and Hastings saw the patrol car in front of him slowing, hesitating, and, shit, the lead patrol car losing it in the turn and slamming into a parked car, the second patrol car hitting its brakes, fishtailing, but holding the turn and then accelerating away. Hastings followed, briefly catching the sight of a white exploded airbag and the flourlike smoke emanating from the smashed car. Hastings kept going.

He heard voices squawking from his radio, calling for assistance now, south on Macklind Avenue, in pursuit of a 1989 Beige Ford Thunderbird, suspect Mike Dillon, armed and dangerous. Heard the call for assist and thought, hurry, man, hurry.

They hit Manchester Road, the same boulevard where it all began, same street but miles farther toward downtown, and the Thunderbird slowed near the intersection because there were sirens and lights approaching from the west, so the Thunderbird turned east and began racing toward Kingshighway, where there would be other patrol cars moving, closing in. . . . The cars driving up an incline now as Kingshighway became a bridge and crossed over a viaduct, railroad tracks beneath.

Dillon saw the lights and siren coming north on Kingshighway. He slowed and cranked the wheel right, descending now into the road before Kingshighway, down toward the railways and the darkness. He took the road two-thirds of the way down the incline, then hit the brakes and cranked the wheel right again, bringing the car to a power slide then a stop. Out of the car then and running as the first police car raced down the incline and T-boned into the Thunderbird.

Dillon kept running.

Hastings had no choice. He stopped the Jag a few feet short of the collision, fully blocking the way. He got out and ran past the patrol car and the Thunderbird. He still had the shotgun.

An eighteen-wheel semi was making a turn at the bottom and coming up the incline. Dillon ran to the right of it and then was alongside of it, the truck and trailer shielding him from a shot.

Hastings had to go to the left of the truck, its gears shifting and motor revving as it began climbing the road . . . slowing as the driver inside saw the collided vehicles in front of him.

Dillon reached the railroad tracks, a classification yard, eighteen to twenty tracks spreading out like a series of fork tines, some with freight cars on them, some not; the Union Pacific and Burlington Northern moved through here alongside trains at a standstill. Dillon moved into the dark cover of it, a forest, and was out of sight by the time Hastings reached the bottom of the incline.

Dillon saw the massive orange locomotive, the hog, pulling a dozen boxcars and a half-dozen flats. He ran in front of its path, plenty of lead time, and moments later heard it pass behind him. The horn blaring after he was already gone, the engineer thinking he was just another transient, squatting in one of the nearby abandoned buildings. The train kept rolling, thacking out a steady beat. Dillon kept running, watching his steps so that he didn't trip. He was in good shape for his age, but he was not a jogger and he was losing wind. He saw a boxcar ahead to his left and ran to it. When he got to the other side, he leaned back against it and tried to rest and think.

Hastings waited for the Union Pacific line to pass by then ran behind it, ran over tracks, then slowed and stopped and looked.

More tracks, railroad cars, dark places where a man could crouch and hide. In the distance he could see Interstate 44, hear its traffic. He looked left and right, moved forward.

Behind the boxcar, Dillon too looked to his left and right. East was the Kingshighway Bridge, darker underneath it. But between this place and the bridge there was a lot of open ground. Police cars had been driving over that bridge only minutes ago. There could be more posted up there, maybe with a searchlight, the advantage of being able to look down on him. To the west, more tracks. Go that way maybe half a mile and the tracks would converge. Less cover, but less light too. There was another boxcar on another track, southwest, maybe forty yards away, open ground between there and here, but he needed to move.

He moved.

And Hastings saw him. Saw him and raised the shotgun and fired. And missed. Hastings racked the slide, but Dillon was behind the boxcar now, putting his hands around the corner, and firing shots from his pistol.

Hastings ran to his left and took cover behind the boxcar Dillon had previously used to hide himself. Two more shots, but Hastings was sheltered then, and Dillon stopped wasting bullets.

Silence.

Hastings waited. Somehow, he knew he should wait.

Five seconds dragged by.

Then he heard the man call out to him.

"Hey," Dillon said. "Hey."

Hastings called back, "What?"

"Did I get you?"

Hastings processed it for a moment. The killer was calling him out. Enjoying it.

"Huh?" Dillon said again. "Did I get you?"

"Yeah," Hastings called back. "Someone needs to call an ambulance."

More silence. Then Hastings heard the man laugh.

"Ah, I didn't get you," Dillon said. "Shit.

Wasted shots."

Hastings said, "You'll get over it."

"Yeah, right. Hey, I know you?"

"No."

"You're metro, aren't you?"

"Yeah."

"Man, what do you guys want with me?"

"Well," Hastings said, "you killed three police officers. Around here, we don't like that."

"You're not clipped. Yet. Why don't you just turn around and go?"

"Maybe I will."

"No, come on, man. Seriously. You got a wife and kids, don't you? Go home and have dinner with them. Go home alive."

Hastings said, "Why don't you come with me? Step out and we'll discuss it."

Dillon looked at the side of the boxcar. There was a rung in front of him, a few feet to his left. A ladder rung running up the side of the car.

"Buddy," Dillon said, "I'm not worth dying over."

Dillon took one hand off his pistol and put it on the rung.

Hastings said, "You're right about that." Hastings began edging away from the corner of his boxcar.

Dillon was climbing the ladder now.

He said, "What's this all about anyway? Salary and a pension? It doesn't mean anything. No one will care, no one will know. Just move on."

Dillon had his hands on the top of the boxcar now. He peered over the edge, made sure it was clear. He climbed on top, stayed down at first. He had seen the cop briefly. Plainclothes, probably a detective. The same one standing by the door with the *what the fuck* expression on his face as Dillon drove the Thunderbird out of the garage. He was talking cool, but had to be scared while he waited for a helicopter or SWAT to show up and bail his ass out.

Dillon got to his knees and looked out over the boxcar. He stood up, put both hands on the pistol.

"All right," Dillon said, "what can you offer me if I surrender?" Waiting now for the cop to step out and look across the yard as Dillon stood over him.

Hastings rounded the second corner of his boxcar and saw the man as he spoke, saw the man standing on top of the boxcar looking, concentrating on the corner where Hastings had been. Hastings raised the shotgun, aimed, and squeezed the trigger.

The shot took Dillon full in the side and

punched him off the boxcar.

Hastings ran around to the other side, pumping another shell in the chamber as he did so, knowing the damage buckshot did at this range but not taking any chances on this one, still hoping it would not be necessary to fire on him again.

It wasn't. Dillon lay on his back, twisted and broken and half of his side cracked open. He had not been able to hold onto his pistol.

Hastings stood over him.

Dillon looked up at him, grinning and gasping, his wound making noises on its own.

Hastings held the shotgun at his side, something taken out of him now.

"God," Dillon said, "I didn't even know you were over there. You part Indian or something?"

Hastings knew there wouldn't be much time. He said, "You shot Cain."

Dillon still gasping. He said, "Which one was he?"

Hastings said nothing. He was tired now. He felt no shame or remorse, but he could not take pleasure in seeing this beast suffer either.

Dillon said, "You sure I don't know you?"

"Yeah," Hastings said. "I'm sure."

"Ohhhh . . . well," Dillon said, "I guess there are worse ways to die."

FORTY-THREE

The nurse told him that he would have to have clothes brought to him when he checked out; his pants and shirt had been cut off in the emergency room. They still had his shoes and his jacket, though there were bloodstains on them both. Regan waited for the nurse or the doctor to tell him the police wanted to talk to him. Neither one of them did. The nurse's assistant was friendly though, smiling at him because he was dangerous and handsome.

Regan had never stayed in a hospital before. He supposed he could sneak out of the room, stand out in the hall in bare ass, and look for some clothes. But he had had his identification on him when he was shot, which he was sure the police had looked at by now, so there wouldn't be much point. He woke up at seven o'clock, the usual time. Except on this morning, the morphine had worn off and he felt like someone had driven over his midsection with a tractor. He found a remote next to his bed and turned the TV on because he couldn't get back to sleep and he told himself that the best plan was to remain cool until he could walk out of here.

That was how he found out Dillon was dead. Shot by the police in a railroad yard sometime in the night. Jimmy was dead too, though he had already known that. He watched images on the screen, a plain-clothes detective walking up an incline toward two wrecked cars, one of them a police cruiser, the detective holding a shotgun with one hand, down at his side.

Jesus, it was done. Mike Dillon, nailed with a shotgun.

Would he have to give his half of the money back to Zans?

The nurse came in with a cup of water and some pain pills and advised him to take them. He did and was asleep in ten minutes.

When he woke up, the sun was brighter in his room. And there was a guy sitting in the visitor's chair. The same guy he had seen on television. Surreal.

Hastings said, "How you feeling?"

Regan said, "Tired."

"Yeah, well, you lost a lot of blood."

Regan said, "Apparently." The cop didn't

have the shotgun with him.

Hastings said, "Planning on going home soon?"

"Hoping to," Regan said. "I'll have to call my wife, have her come get me."

"Don't feel up to driving?"

"No."

Hastings said, "Planning on taking the gun back with you?"

"What gun?"

"The one found in your jacket after you passed out," Hastings said. "It's not registered to you, but then they never are, are they?"

Regan shrugged.

"Still," Hastings said, "it's got your prints all over it."

"So what?"

"So nothing," Hastings said. "It's a misdemeanor I'll stretch into a felony. Or not. I haven't decided. I'm tired. Maybe I need to sleep too." Hastings sighed. "I spent the last few hours on the telephone with Chicago police. They told me who you are, what you do."

"I own a bar. We serve food as well."

Hastings went on as if he hadn't heard him. "Three people in Chicago killed in the last few days, three cops killed here. Nice little balance. Two of them killed in your place. One of them the brother of Jimmy Rizza."

Regan shrugged. "I wasn't there. Ask anyone."

"I don't need to ask; I know. Anyway, what you did in Chicago is Chicago's business. What you did here is mine."

"I got shot here. You want me to register a complaint with you?"

"You're an assassin. Killer for the mob. They say you're the man they call to take care of snitches."

"Do they."

"And that's what I think you were here for. To take care of Jimmy Rizza and Michael Dillon."

"Well, it didn't happen, did it?"

"No, things don't turn out like you plan," Hastings said. "But I would like to know who sent you here."

Regan smiled, said nothing.

"Who put the hit out on Dillon and Rizza?"

"Hit? What do you — *I* got hit."

"Who was protecting Dillon?"

"I can't help you," Regan said. "You got charges to file, file 'em."

"*Was* Dillon a snitch?"

Regan shrugged again. He said, "Clean your own house."

"I'm trying," Hastings said.

After a moment, Regan said, "Sean would have known."

Hastings looked at Regan. Regan picked up the remote and turned on the television. Sound and light interfering now.

Hastings said, "Sean Rizza?"

Regan nodded.

"But he's dead."

Regan kept his eyes on the television. He said, "You're the detective." It was all he was going to say.

FORTY-FOUR

Rhodes was waiting for him in the coffee shop of the hospital lobby. Hastings acknowledged him and said he needed to get some coffee. He was hungry too; a tired hungry, but the prepackaged "big donut" looked too big and sugary at this hour. He wondered if they had a toaster and some plain white bread in the back, because a couple of slices of lightly buttered toast would work just fine. But he realized that it would be silly to ask. He took his coffee and sat at the small beige table with Rhodes.

Rhodes said, "Well?"

Hastings said, "He's a lifer."

"What do you mean?"

"A professional criminal. Probably most of his life. Chicago PD said he was clever. Never spent any time in prison. Never ratted on anyone in the mob to stay out of prison."

"So?"

"So he didn't manage that by telling cops what they want to know. He's not going to tell us that, yes, he was sent here by the mob to whack Mike Dillon." Hastings sighed. "He knows we know already. So why give us anything?"

"But you took care of Dillon for him."

"So what?"

"So," Rhodes said, "maybe he's grateful."

"His is not a grateful lifestyle. Still," Hastings said, "he did say we should check out Sean Rizza."

"Sean Rizza?" Rhodes said, "Wasn't he one of the guys that was killed in Regan's bar?"

"Yeah," Hastings said, "it is funny."

A couple of nurses in scrubs took a table nearby. The one in pink scrubs told the other not to get her started because she was having the worst day. The other said, okay, and let her explain things.

Rhodes said, "George?"

"Yeah?"

"Why don't you go home?"

"Why?"

"May I say this with all respect?"

"Go ahead."

"What difference does it make?" Rhodes said. "What difference does it make who sent Regan here? We got Dillon and Rizza.

Those are our guys. Let Chicago handle Jack Regan."

Hastings rubbed his eyes. "It isn't about Regan," he said.

"What?"

"It isn't about Regan."

"Then what is it? You want to pull Dillon out of the morgue, get him to confess?"

"I tell you, I would if I could."

"But to what? If you're wondering about Cain, it's about as solid a case as you're going to get. Didn't he say to you, 'Which one was he?' Or something similar? And the woman, didn't she tell you that he killed Hummel? And Murph's statement: he was there. He saw Dillon. You read it yourself."

"I know."

"Then what? What, George?"

Hastings was looking at the large bagel with cream cheese sitting on the nurse's table. Big enough for two to eat.

Hastings said, "You're right."

"Lieutenant, it's your call. But you've been up all night. And I think you should sleep. At least for a couple of hours."

"Howard," Hastings said, "you're making sense."

A couple of hours sounded good. So he set the alarm for two hours and did some rounding up and it went off at 11:45 a.m. The radio was set on KMOX and he heard jumbles of conversation forming into Rush Limbaugh, talking about the hypocrisy of some other guy who had a talk show on television. Hastings turned the radio off. He sat up in bed and put his feet on the floor.

And then he said, "Clean my own house?"

He was driving on I-64 when he got Rhodes on the phone.

"Howard? It's George."

"You get some sleep?"

"Yeah. Did a world of good. Listen, in the hospital, Regan said something that I didn't give much thought to until now. He said, 'Clean your own house.'"

"Yeah?" Rhodes wasn't following him yet, but he was willing to be patient.

"Well," Hastings said, "I said some stupid shit like 'I'm trying,' but I wasn't really thinking clearly at the time. I thought he meant, clean it up on your own. But he was talking about something else."

"Like?"

"Cops. Law enforcement. Clean your own house, don't worry about mine."

"But Treats said the same thing. How is this different?"

"It is different. Regan had nothing to do

with Hummel. He was after Dillon."

"Because Dillon was a snitch," Rhodes said. "We know that now."

"But we've been looking at it backwards, Howard. We've been looking at who he snitched on when *we should have been looking at who he snitched to.*"

"Why?"

"Because Chicago PD told us yesterday that someone tipped off Dillon before he could be arrested, but they don't know who. And what Regan was telling me this morning was that that someone was in law enforcement."

"He actually said that?"

"He didn't say it directly, Howard. But there has to be a connection. There has to be."

There was a silence. And Hastings wondered if he'd lost his signal.

"Howard?"

"Yeah, I'm here. Who did Regan say we should look into?"

"Sean Rizza."

"I'll start placing calls," Rhodes said.

Hastings said, "I'll be there in ten minutes."

FORTY-FIVE

The owner of the restaurant was standing at their table, hand on his hip, laughing and joking with them. The men at the table trying a wine the owner had recommended as he talked about a small farm outside of Verona where he had grown up.

Frank was enjoying himself. Holding court with three other agents, all junior to him, looking up the Special Agent in Charge with his well-cut suit and broad shoulders. Sharing wine and war stories. Frank felt good. He had seen it on the news this morning, listened to the story again as he drove to work, and he could not believe his good fortune. Jimmy and Mike dead, both of them killed. He was free now, released from the devil's pact he had formed with the two of them over the years. *Free.*

He shared his good humor with the agents from his office, all of them younger than him, all of them willing to flatter him. It was an insincere affection and respect, but one that he accepted as real. The owner placing a hand on Frank's shoulder as he looked at the other three agents and said, "Watch out for this guy, eh?" the agents smiling and laughing on cue.

The owner left them and returned to the bar.

Frank said, "He's a character." Frank liked calling people characters. Sometimes he called them rascals. He liked to drink wine and have dinner and be seen at places like this.

One of the agents said, "Frank, you're going to die of boredom after you retire."

"Golf," Frank said. "I plan to watch a lot of it."

Another agent said, "That or run for congress."

"Not enough money in that," a third agent said.

"Hey," Frank said, "I don't need much. I'm civil service."

The laughter ebbed as one of the agents became aware of another man's presence. Standing at the table now as the agents stopped talking and looked.

Frank said, "Can I help you, friend?"

Hastings said, "Yeah, are you Frank Cahalin?"

"Yes."

Hastings extended his hand. "George Hastings. I'm a lieutenant with St. Louis PD."

"Oh, hey," Frank said, shaking the hand. "How you doing?"

Hastings shook his head, smiling. "Tired," he said.

One of the agents said, "Hastings?"

"Yeah."

The agent said, "Are you the cop that — ?"

Hastings nodded.

"Holy shit," the agent said. "This is the guy that brought down the cop killer last night. Sit down, will you? Let us buy you a drink."

"Well . . ."

"Come on."

"Okay," Hastings said. "Just for a minute."

Frank said, "Good work, George."

Hastings shrugged.

An agent said, "Got him with a shotgun, huh?"

"Yeah."

"Man, that's great," another agent said. "That guy needed to die."

"Yeah, I guess so." Hastings glanced just briefly at Cahalin when he said it.

Another agent said, "You need to take

some time off, man. Get laid." He laughed but no one else joined him.

Hastings smiled briefly. He said, "So about when was it that you went native?" He was looking at Frank when he finished saying it, his expression patient, his voice calm.

Frank said, "Pardon me?"

Hastings said, "When would you say it was?"

"When I went . . . I'm sorry," Frank said, "I don't understand your question."

"Was it five years ago? Ten years ago? When?"

"Uh, George," Frank said, smiling now, "you got to clue me in to what you're talking about."

Hastings said, "Did you take money from him? Or was it something else? A girl? An affair with a homosexual? Come on, you can tell us."

Frank said, "Man, what planet are you on? Take money from who, Lieutenant?" Frank was using his impatient supervisor's tone now, asserting himself.

But it wasn't working. Not with this man.

"From Mike Dillon," Hastings said. "The man who murdered three police officers. In case anyone here has forgotten."

One of the agents started to say something, but stopped.

Frank was aware of the agents watching him. Challenged now by the plainclothes metro detective, the detective trying to ambush him in a public place. Frank said, "George? You lost one of your men, so I understand your being upset. Tired too. But if you think you can walk in here —"

Hastings said, "You make one more reference to Robert Cain, I'll tear your head off."

The agents at the table saw the fierce, almost crazy look in the detective's eyes and, for just a second, saw Frank's chin tremble and his hands shake. And that brief moment told them that Frank Cahalin was not quite ruthless enough to be a hardened criminal, not quite smart enough to be a practiced con artist.

Frank said, "I think you better leave, before you commit career suicide."

Hastings leaned back in his chair, put aside his desire to smash the fed in his fat face. "You see," Hastings said, "we're not quite as dumb as you think we are. Us metro people, that is. There are some pretty smart people in the Department, actually. Some not as smart as others. But I'll tell you something, Frank, I never met anybody in the department dumb enough to be played by Mike Dillon. I mean, they'd see him for what he was. A turd. A killer. You, you befriended him. I think on some level, you even came to admire him."

"You don't know what you're talking about."

"He helped you, right? I understand that. We all use informants we wouldn't want near our homes. It's part of the work. He helped you rise in the ranks, got you out of handling insurance fraud cases, helped you put some Sicilians in prison. But didn't you see, Frank? Didn't you see what he was doing? Did you pretend not to see it? You had to know. *He was using you,* using you to put his competitors in jail and get himself the protection of the biggest law enforcement agency in the country."

Frank said, "You're talking about things you don't know anything about. Things you can't possibly understand. It's beyond your world of dopers and pimps and domestic assault. You're just talking to talk. You don't have anything."

Hastings said, "Sean Rizza."

"Yeah?" Frank said. "What about him?"

"Five years ago, a bookie was beaten to death in the back of a tavern. There was a fair amount of evidence Sean had done it with a baseball bat. Cook County DA convened a grand jury to investigate it. A

367

week later, it was yanked."

"So what?"

"This afternoon, I called the district attorney's office to find out what happened. They told me the DA was busy, but I could leave a message." Hastings paused. "So I called the assistant DA who was working the case to see what she knew. It took her awhile, but she found this."

Hastings removed a faxed copy of a letter from his jacket pocket. He read it aloud. "Dear Mr. Ahrens, please be advised that this office is deeply disappointed that time and resources are being expended to target Sean Rizza in the above investigation. Mr. Rizza has assisted this office in efforts to combat organized criminal activity. Furthermore, it is well known that the deceased was recently paroled from prison and had a history of violent criminal behavior. Mr. Rizza, in contrast, is a respected businessman and a man I personally believe to be of good moral character. Sincerely, Frank Cahalin, Special Agent, Federal Bureau of Investigation."

The three agents looked from Hastings to Frank.

Frank said, "Yeah, I wrote that. So what?"

"Sean Rizza's dead now, you know that."

"Yeah, I know. You going to piss on his

grave too?"

"Well, I think most law enforcement officers in Chicago would dispute the part about Sean Rizza's good moral character. I think you wrote that letter because Mike Dillon asked you to. Or told you. But maybe you're right. Maybe it's nothing," Hastings said. "But then there are those phone records."

Frank was looking at him.

"Yeah," Hastings said, "we decided to subpoena your phone records to see if you'd been in touch with Dillon. You were. But that's not all. Much to our surprise, we found out that you called Sergeant Cain on his cell phone from your office about thirty-five minutes before he was killed. Then another call was placed, from your office, to the home of Jerry Rosinski, aka Mike Dillon. From your office, ten minutes later. Now, maybe you didn't think to use a pay phone for that second call because you were dumb. But my guess is, you panicked. Cain told you where he was going because he could be careless with people in positions of authority. He was a good detective and, in his way, a pretty good man, but he put a little too much stock in people like you. You panicked and you called Dillon and you told him Cain was going to see Sharon Dunphy.

Whether you intended it or not, you got Cain killed."

Frank opened his mouth. "I —"

Hastings held up a hand. "Don't say anything, Frank. Just — don't."

The agents were aware now of the quiet in the restaurant and several uniformed city cops standing nearby, a black plainclothes officer with them. Approaching now as Hastings got up and walked away.

Rhodes said, "Frank Cahalin. Stand up. You're under arrest."

Hastings walked out into the night, crossed the street, and got into his car. He started the car, hesitated as he reached for the gearshift. He stopped and put his hands on the steering wheel and gripped it. He felt his blood thrumming, his adrenaline still racing.

Back there in that restaurant, he had wanted to kill that man. Had wanted to put him against a wall and shoot him. He knew he was capable of it and it frightened him. If asked, he would not be able to explain his anger. If he had felt this sort of anger before, he could not remember when. He had not felt it when his wife betrayed him and left him and split up the family. He had not even felt it when he was chasing the gangster through the train yard. But he felt it when he had told Agent Cahalin not to say anything more, and he was glad he lived in a time when the law prevented him from taking a life so easily.

He sat with his hands on the wheel for a few more minutes until he decided it had passed and he felt tired more than anything. Then he reached for his cell phone, dialed a number, and waited.

"Hello?"

"Hi. It's George. George Hastings."

"Oh, hi," Carol said. "Hi. What's going on?"

"It's wrapped up. My part of it, anyway."

"I was going to call you," she said. "I saw it on the news. What you did, I mean."

"Yeah."

"Are you all right?"

"Yeah, I'm okay."

"You weren't hurt?"

"No."

"The other police officer," she said. "I'm sorry."

"Yeah," Hastings said. "I think the funeral is Monday." He wasn't sure what else to say right now. "Listen, I'm sorry, I know we're not — I just wanted to talk to someone, that's all. Maybe we could meet for a cup of coffee or something."

"You sound tired."

"Yeah, I am, I guess."

There was a silence. He did not want to tell her what he had been thinking. He was not sure he would ever tell anyone.

Carol said, "George?"

"Yes."

"Are you still there?"

"Yes, I'm sorry."

She said, "Why don't you come over? I can make you some coffee here."

Hastings said, "I'd like that."

ABOUT THE AUTHOR

James Patrick Hunt, a lawyer, was born in Surrey, England. He graduated from St. Louis University and Marquette University Law School and is the author of three previous novels. This is his first novel featuring George Hastings. Hunt now lives in Tulsa, Oklahoma.